TEN YEARS IN THE PEN HAD BROKEN BERT WILLARD.

All the fight and courage that had once caused people to call him "the Chief" had gone out of him. When he had first gone to prison, he had laughed at the rules, bucked his jailers. But the assistant warden told Bert that he'd break him, make him get down on his knees and crawl to him and beg his pardon.

Bert was sure he could stand beatings—burnings, even. He could stand ten years of bread and water, and still damn them all to their faces. But they didn't use starving or flogging.

They just put him in the dark. In solitary. In the end he got down on his knees—and crawled. And when they let him out of prison, he thought he could never fight again.

Until the day came when Bert Willard had to find his courage—or let his brother die. . . .

WARNER BOOKS
By Max Brand

MAX BRAND

Brothers on The Trail

WARNER BOOKS

A Warner Communications Company

This Warner Books Edition is published by
arrangement with Dodd, Mead & Company, Inc.,
79 Madison Avenue, N.Y., N.Y.

Warner Books, Inc.
666 Fifth Avenue
New York, N.Y. 10103

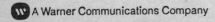 A Warner Communications Company

Printed in the United States of America

First Warner Books Printing: April, 1972

Reissued: April, 1986

10 9 8 7 6 5

CHAPTER I

THE NO. 1 MAN

EVERYBODY called my brother "Chief" or "The Chief," and when he came home after being away for ten years, and spending three of them in prison, he was as much of a "Big Indian" as ever, around our part of the range. His record didn't matter. For seven years, he'd climbed all over the cattle country raising the devil, and the devil that he raised seemed likely to stay above ground, too. He'd stuck up stagecoaches and robbed a bank, and a ton of other things were laid to him, not counting thirty or forty gun fights that always saw him the top dog. But none of these things seemed to matter, because he was "The Chief."

I mean, he'd always been the No. 1 man, wherever he went. He could ride better and rope better, run better, dance better, sing better than any one else. People used to say that the calves liked to have him put the branding iron on them. And when it came to breaking tough mustangs, he seemed to talk them into sense and manners. You know how some people are. They're never wrong, and every situation seems made to order to show their talents. That was the way with the Chief. When he left home—he was only eighteen, then—and began to get in fights every week or so, people simply said:

"Well, the Chief was born to shoot quick and shoot straight. That's the only trouble with him."

Everybody knew that he had gathered a gang of roughs around him and that they were doing the sort of work that isn't paid for, day by day. But they excused that, too. They used to say that he was born into the wrong age. He should have lived in the days of knights and armor, and that sort of thing.

And when at last he was cornered up at Windover

5

Canyon, and they gave him fourteen years in the penitentiary, every one groaned and said the law was too severe. By that time there were fourteen or fifteen dead men laid to his account, and though I guess all the fellows he'd bumped off had been thugs and yeggs, still that's a pretty long list to have against you. But nobody minded. "Youth and high spirits, and too many gifts from God Almighty," they would say.

It turned out that when he went to prison he didn't like the way that prison was run, and he raised the devil there, too. Which, in the wind-up, is the main point about this story. But I didn't find out the meaning until later on. All that my mother and I knew was that the governor of the State had visited that prison, one day, and seeing the Chief, he began to admire the looks of him, and about ten words spoken in the Chief's soft voice were enough to make the governor decide that a terrible injustice would be done if that young man were left inside the penitentiary another day.

That was how Bert happened to come home.

It was a great day. Ten years before, I had been twelve, and I'd hardly had a look at him since, though he'd made some visits by night to see our mother. But ten years can't dim the memory of a fellow like the Chief. Everything that went wrong with me went right with him.

The hair that's flame-colored on my head is softened down to a luster of auburn and gold for the Chief. All the blue was used up on his eyes, and only a pale wash was left for mine. Most of the nose material went into his fine, straight beak, and just a turned-up button was thumbed onto my face. His body was handmade, the sort of a thing that the Creator might have lingered over, admiring His own work. But He made me at the end of the day, I suppose, and just threw together a chunk of material, and roughed it off and said: "To-morrow will be another day."

While they called Bert the "Chief," people called me

6

almost anything, from "Red" to "Shorty," or "Stub," or "Stubby," or "Mug," and my own name of Rickie wasn't used a great deal outside of my family, not even by the girls. And as for Richard, which I was christened, I think I've heard it not more than half a dozen times, and those were all ceremonial occasions.

Well, it was a fine thing to have the Chief back with us. We knew, a few days before, that he was coming. The papers carried a long lot of articles about what he was and what he had been. And the governor sent a telegram to my mother that must have gained him ten thousand votes in the next election. That's the trouble with governors and such; you never can tell where the man leaves off and the politician begins.

I worked a week and cleaned up the buckboard, and slicked up a pair of bay mustangs we had, because the Chief was one to like things fixed up, and he always put the best foot forward. I met him at the station. But do you think that I had a chance to grab him and scoot off home with him? Not at all. The whole town was there, it seemed to me.

All of his friends had turned out, of course, and those who had been his enemies were on hand, too, trying to act pleasant, because they knew that it wasn't the safest thing in the world for them to remain enemies with such a man as the Chief, particularly now that he was no longer an outlaw but able to go anywhere in the open day.

I tell you what, it was a sight to see the Chief step around among those people, giving everybody his voice and eyes, and his handclasp and full smile, one after another, and sort of dwelling on each one for half a second, as though that was the one particular person he'd been thinking about all during the three years that he was in prison. That was the Chief's way. He couldn't help it. He didn't mean to be hypocritical, but he'd been given that face, that voice, those eyes, and most of all, that smile; and it's a shame not to use the gifts of God, so to speak.

7

They got the Chief up on their shoulders and carried him around to a pair of the biggest saloons. There was such a crowd that it overflowed into the street, each time, and the doors had to be propped open, and the glasses passed out by the dozen.

Steve McIntosh, that ran the Golden Hour Saloon, let all the drinks be on the house. I guess it must have cost him a half barrel of his best rye. Steve made a name for himself, that day. It wasn't like a bartender to set up the drinks that way—and for a Scotchman it wasn't hardly natural.

I noticed that the Chief held onto his glass each time, and only drank one drink in each saloon. And I knew why. The minute he was out of prison, he was in danger. Almost any of the men in that crowd might take a crack at him. And there was always sure to be some fool of a young devil that wanted to make a name for himself, and get famous by shooting down a really celebrated gunman like the Chief.

In each of those saloons, the Chief stood on a chair and made a little speech, in which he said words like this: "Partners, I'm out of jail, and it's time to make good resolutions, but I won't act as though it were New Year's. I'm going to try to be the same as always—without stepping on any one's toes."

Well, of course he *couldn't* be the same as before unless he stepped on somebody's toes. I thought of that, and it gave me a comfort, though I laughed with all the rest. But I was glad when I had the Chief safely in the buckboard, at last, and we were rattling out of Buffalo Junction with the dust spinning up into a cloud from the four wheels, and the near mustang trotting, and the off one bearing out and loping, and trying to buck, and acting the fool in general the way some mustangs are born to be.

The Chief didn't talk much. He was one of those fellows who can be silent for a long time, and it's just as though they were talking all the while. He put his hand on my shoulder and left it there, lightly. But somehow I

8

could feel the strength come out of the tips of his fingers and go like electricity all through my body.

He asked about the ranch, very particularly. We didn't have a very big ranch, but before my father died he had worked up a good grade of cattle. And we'd managed to keep the grade just right—not too rough to lose out on the weight or the quality of the beef, and not too fine to take the fighting edge off the steers, the fight that carries beef through hard winters and long droughts. We just about got along, and a little bit more. But the fences and everything were running down a good bit, because there was a lot too much for me to do, and not quite enough to make us hire an extra man. I told the Chief how everything was going, and he seemed much interested. Then I asked:

"What are you going to do, Chief?"

"Ought you to call me that, Rickie?" he asked. "How about 'Bert,' or anything else you want? Do you think you ought to call me 'Chief'?"

I only laughed.

"You'll be the Chief for me, all the time," said I. "You'll never be anything else, because you're the Big Indian for me, old son!"

"All right," said the Chief. He patted my shoulder, once or twice. There seemed to be a sort of sadness in his smile.

Then I asked him again what he was going to do, and he said:

"I wonder if you'd mind if I stayed on at the ranch for a while, Rickie? I mean, working along with you."

I jumped almost out of the buckboard.

"You mean working cows—just like an ordinary cow-puncher?"

He smiled at me, and looked me over quietly, from the chin to the eyes, and back again.

"That's what I mean," he said. "The most ornery of ordinary cow-punchers. Do you mind if I stay here?"

"Why, Chief," I shouted, "where would you be welcome to stay, except on your own place?"

9

He frowned. The smile jerked off his face in an instant. He shook his head, as he answered: "Look here, Rickie. Understand me, now, because I'm not going to keep talking about it."

The way he said this overawed me. I was silent, and gaped at him. He went on:

"I'd like to stay on at the ranch, for a while, at least, trying to freshen up on handling horses and cattle, and everything that a ranchman ought to know and do. But mind you, the place is yours. I went away when you were a kid of twelve, and you've had a tough time for ten years to keep things going. Shut up, now, and don't interrupt me. Maybe I did send in some money, now and then, but not enough. And it wasn't money that came in the right way, either. You've fought for that ranch for ten years, and it's yours. Heaven help my wretched soul if I ever claim an acre of it!"

A shudder went through him. And as I looked at him, then, I saw a shadow rush out of his eyes. I hate to put it that way, because I know it doesn't sound right, but that's what I mean—a shadow came flooding out of his eyes, and not the usual sparkling light. And I knew, in that instant, that something had happened to the Chief, and that he was not the man he used to be.

I couldn't spot the change, exactly. It might be sorrow, or pain, or hard memories, or the loss of something he had loved. I couldn't spot the change, but it was there, all right. And I felt so cold and sick that I wasn't able to protest about the way he was giving up his claim to the home place.

When we got there. I stood around in corners, and watched mother devour the Chief. It was the same old story. She was always petting him—touching him when she went by him, smoothing his hair, brushing a bit of dust or lint off his coat, loving him with her eyes. He detested it, as he always had detested it. And just as always, he endured it and managed to keep on smiling.

Mother was my cut, more or less—dark-skinned and flaming hair. The gray had not put out the fire in it, as

10

yet. My father had been a noble-looking fellow, fond of his mustache. His pictures always showed him in attitudes. The Chief was like father—without the attitudes, because he was the most natural, graceful, fine-looking man that I ever laid an eye on.

In the case of mother and father, I suppose it was the attraction of opposites. But in the case of mother and the Chief, there was a repulsion. She worshiped him; she hungered for him; she smiled and laughed like a girl, or brooded over him as though he were still a baby. But the Chief could hardly endure it, and he was always cutting these fond scenes short and slipping away, and leaving mother with nothing but my mug to look at.

Even that first day, it was the same thing over again, and the Chief was not happy until he had a chance to get out with me, and climb into old clothes, and then ride out on the range. I played a bit of a joke on him, and gave him the worst tough-mouthed mustang on the place, and the meanest broncho when it came to pitching. It used to take me a half hour to work the kinks out of that spooky devil. But in half a minute the Chief had the brute in the palm of his hand, and rode him with a loose rein, as though the beast had a mouth of silk.

It may sound to you like a small thing, but I was filled with awe. It tickled me to the marrow, and it almost knocked me out of my saddle, too.

We rode all over our range, and I could see that his eye was noticing everything that was wrong—the big white alkali spot that had appeared in the hollow, and the broken wall of the "tank" that had washed out in the spring rains, and all the loose, sagging bits of fence, with patched-up and rusted barbed wire. However, no matter what he saw, he said nothing about it. And it was a happy day for me. I'd slide my eye over him and wonder how I'd been able to live alone on this range, when I had such a brother in the world. It just didn't seem possible.

We got in just in time for supper, and it was a whale

of a meal. The Chief made all the conversation, while Mother and I sat back and drank up him and his talk. But twice or three times, in pauses, he looked straight before him, at nothing, and I saw the darkness flood out of his eyes again. Mother noticed nothing, but I knew that there was trouble, terrible trouble in the air.

CHAPTER II

HAPPY DAYS

I was right. There was terrible trouble in the air, and of a sort that I never could have dreamed of. I hate to write about it. I prefer to linger a while on those happy, happy days when the Chief and I were riding the range together.

He took hold right away. Everything was changed. Everything began to pick up. I give you my word that in three days some of the sick cattle began to get well. And the whole place, in a week, looked as though some mechanic had been working on it for a year. The fences began to be tighter and straighter; the posts no longer were wabbling. Because, though he never seemed to hurry, the Chief made every stroke of his hands count. And he could do three things at once. He could ride herd, build fence, and doctor cattle all at the same time, turning from one job to the next, economizing movements, and getting through in one day what would have taken me four.

He seemed to be out for any sort of work that would make a little honest money, too. When people dropped in to see him, for instance, they soon got in the habit of fetching along their worst outlaws. And he'd take those bronchos that couldn't give any satisfaction except in the way of breaking necks or pitching at rodeos, and inside of a week, he'd have them so a woman could ride them—a range woman, I mean, of course. He used to get ten dollars a head, or even fifteen, for that sort of work.

12

My mother and I were amazed to see how he piled up the coin—simply by riding those nags for a little while in the evening, or during the lunch hour, and never interfering with the main program of work in the least.

He found time, too, to teach me a lot of things that I wanted to learn. He knew how to throw a rope underhand, like a Mexican. But that was too hard for me. He knew how to throw a knife, too, so that it was more deadly than a revolver in the hands of most men. But the knife was too hard for me. I couldn't master it at all. However, I picked up some tricks about riding, and how to handle the reins so that a horse knows it has its master on its back, but not its hard-handed enemy. Above all, he showed me a lot of gun tricks.

He always had to have a revolver with him, of course, because seeing what he had been, enemies might crop up in the middle of the field, at any time. He wore a Colt as the slickest gunmen usually do—in a spring holster under the pit of the left arm. Or, if he went double-heeled, under the pits of both arms. The sights were filed off them, so that the draw would be surer and faster. The triggers were filed off, and he fired with a flick of his thumb, because in that way a skillful fellow can turn a revolver into a burst of machine-gun fire.

He taught me a lot about that art. You only have five shots in a gun, because the hammer has to rest on an empty chamber—considering the hair-trigger effect. But when you learn how to use the Colt, in that system, you can make ten shots roll off in about two seconds, and with practice you can blow the tar out of short-range targets. You don't aim by sighting, but by the sense of pointing.

A man like the Chief could plug half dollars two times but of three at ten yards. I never got as good as that. I lacked the gift. But I could plaster a man-sized stump at any barroom distance, or even as far as across the street.

But no matter what I tried to do, I never had the same ease and fluency of my brother. Not in anything except in swearing, which was a talent that he didn't possess at all.

Well, I like to linger on those days, perhaps because there were so few of them.

Most of the evenings, the Chief was at home. But after a couple of weeks, mother insisted that he should go out to a dance, because she said that fine birds cannot be kept in small cages. So the Chief and I drove over to Farmington together to the Saturday night dance. We scrubbed down with yellow laundry soap at the end of the day's work, and had an early supper, and drove over.

It was a thing to make you laugh, to see the way that the Chief ran his eyes over the girls and then picked out the best of the lot. That was Allardyce Benchley. She looked like her name, too. I mean, you'd think that on the range she'd be called "Al," for short. But not at all. She was good-natured, she never played favorites, and she wasn't a bit of a snob, but she could be cool, too. She was never really what you'd call a "good fellow." But she had looks—a ton of them.

She was so pretty that she made your heart bump twice at the same spot in your throat, when you looked at her. The boys all liked her, but we were all afraid of her. Particularly because she had all of her father's money behind her, and Jerome Benchley was one of the cattle kings. That is, he was "Jerome Benchley" in the newspapers, and "Jerry Benchley" outside of them. He *was* a right hearty old buck.

Well, he was there that night. And about half an hour after the Chief had slipped in to a corner and taken Allardyce out of a mêlée of cowhands who wanted a dance—half an hour after that, when it was pretty clear that Allardyce could see only one face and hear only one voice—Jerry Benchley pulled up beside me and said:

"I hope he'll marry the girl!"

I grinned at him, but he was *not* grinning, just then.

He chewed one end of his mustache and swore, and he didn't do his swearing under his breath either.

There were two shows, that evening. There was the band, and all the rest of the crowd; and then there was that couple—the Chief and Allardyce. He brought her over, and they stood with me between dances, once.

"Nobody else has a brother," said the Chief. "I've got the only real one."

He never praised me. I suppose he knew that it did something funny to my insides when he said pleasant things. I got red and happy, and Allardyce shone her eyes at me, and then melted them at me. She didn't look like a girl who has just met a man. She looked as though it were her wedding night, by thunder. She looked at me as though I already had a right to sit at her table! And she asked about mother!

A while after that came a crash. It was out in the cloakroom, where sombreros and things were hung around the walls, and where the men went to smoke, now and then. The Chief had just stepped out, smiling at everybody he passed as though he wanted to stop and speak to them. He had just made and lighted a cigarette when "Bingo" Walters came up with a drawn face that had a hard ridge on each side of the mouth, and a white streak in the middle of the cheek.

"I want to talk to you, Chief," said he.

"About what, old son?" asked my brother.

"About trouble," said Bingo, sticking out his chin.

"Not about trouble!" said the Chief. "I hate to talk about trouble!"

He pretended to catch a puff of his smoke in his hand, and throw it at Bingo.

You could hear yourself think, by this time. Then somebody said:

"Bingo, are you drunk? Know who you're talking to?"

Bingo made a half hitch around and said: "Shut your mouth. I know whom I'm talking to. I'm reminding you Chief, that I signed up to dance that last dance with

15

Allardyce Benchley. I want to know what you mean by stealing it?"

I held my breath, but the lightning did not strike. The Chief simply said:

"I didn't know you had the dance. Perhaps I've stolen other things—but not dances, Bingo."

Bingo had taken the dive toward a fight, and he wouldn't back up, though you could see that he expected to be smashed to bits. Some men are that way. They'd rather die than have anything put over on them.

"I missed that last dance," he said, "and I'm going to have the next one."

"That," said the Chief, "is something for you and Allardyce Benchley to work out together." He kept his voice gentle.

"No," said Bingo, raging, "*you* can work it out for me—you seem to own her."

I backed up against the wall, and my stomach muscles hardened. I thought that the guns would flash that instant. Bingo thought so, too. He leaned forward a little, his weight on his toes, his arms crooked up so that he looked like a wrestler about to dive in for a hold.

I stared at the Chief. Someone was beginning to moan with fear. The Chief was very pale. And again, out of his eyes, I saw the blank darkness pouring. Then he said, softly, so that I could hardly hear him:

"I'm going outside."

"Are you inviting me to come out there with you?" shouted Bingo.

"No," said the Chief. "I'm not doing that. I want to be alone."

And he walked straight out the door into the darkness.

I began to breathe again. Bingo, looking sick and weak after the strain of taking his life in his hands for the sake of what he considered his self-respect, leaned a hand against the wall, and trembled all over.

Old Benchley appeared from nowhere.

16

"That was a mighty fine thing," he said. "You can thank Heaven that you're still alive, Bingo. If *I* were you, I'd go out and ask the pardon of that—gentleman!"

It was the way he said the last word that counted.

Bingo looked up sideways at Benchley.

"Yeah," he said. "You're right. I was a fool. I'm going to go out and ask his pardon right now!"

He went, too. And we could hear his voice barking out the words loudly, so that everybody could be in on his humiliation, just as everybody could have been in on the fight. Then I heard the easy, musical voice of the Chief. Presently they came arm in arm to the door. But Bingo couldn't face the rest of us. He'd done his bit and so now he faded out and left the party.

But I was left thinking about nothing but the terrible, empty eyes of my brother.

CHAPTER III

A BLOOD TRAIL

AFTER that, the Chief wanted to go home. I felt the reason was that he thought he had been made too conspicuous, because everybody was standing about commenting on his good nature and presence of mind in refusing to use his superior hand in wiping out Bingo. The Chief went back and danced one more dance, but after that, he gave me a high sign. A lot of couples went out to stroll around and get the cool of the air between dances; and this time, Allardyce Benchley came out with the Chief.

I knew what the high sign meant, so I got the team ready and drove up for the Chief to get in. Allardyce was still with him, and by that time Jerome Benchley was with the pair of them. Every time he turned toward the gasoline lamp over the entrance of the dance hall, I could see the shine of the big diamond he wore in his necktie. He was saying in his huge voice:

"What about this, Chief? You act as though you aimed to run away with Al, here! What about it?"

"One day I'm going to try," said the Chief, with his smile.

"I'll be ready," said Allardyce, with never a smile at all.

I leaned out of the buckboard and kind of gloried in her, her beauty and all, and the shine of her hair, and the way she was giving herself with her eyes to the Chief.

Benchley broke it with: "What the devil kind of nonsense is this? Al, are you making a fool of yourself?"

"Am I making a fool of myself, Chief?" asked Allardyce.

Benchley turned his back on them with a groan.

"They're serious!" he said. He seemed to be talking to me, but he wasn't.

They kept a silence while he was turned away. They were standing close together, she with her head up, and he with his head down in a way that told everything.

"Chief," said Benchley, turning suddenly around again, "you've been a worthless sort of a scatter-brained, fly-by-night chipmunk, always falling into love and out again. Are you flirting or serious? I'm going to find out, because I've never seen Al like this, before. Al, have you ever been like this, before?"

Instead of answering her father, she smiled up at the Chief.

"Damn!" said Benchley. "It looks like the real old-fashioned poison. Chief, come here!"

"All right," said the Chief, without budging out of his trance.

Benchley stepped up to them.

"They tell me that you're making a good start out on your place," he said. "They tell me that you're settling down. But it don't take much to scare a wild hawk off the nest, does it?"

"No," said the Chief.

"All I say is," went on Benchley, "I expect you'll play

18

fair. You won't be swift or sudden, or anything like that?"

The Chief pulled his eyes away from Allardyce and laid them on Benchley.

"No," he said, in a way that made Benchley put a hand on his arm and give it a grip.

"You run along home," said Benchley. "You did a good job, to-night, to keep from massacring that young fool of a Bingo Walters. And I'll take Al home, too, because it looks as though she has something to think over. Chief, if you have nothing to do on Sunday, come along and shove your feet under our table for dinner."

"Thanks," said the Chief. "I'll come. Good-by, Allardyce." He took her hand.

"Good night, Chief," said she.

"Well, kiss her, then!" exclaimed Benchley.

And that's what the Chief did, though I suppose fifty people had stopped stock-still under the pines, by this time, and were looking on from a distance. There wasn't much light, but there was enough. I was still a little dizzy after the Chief got into the buckboard and drove away with me.

He took the reins out of my hands and put those mustangs into their best trot. For me they were always half trotting, half loping, half bucking, if you understand what I mean, but for the Chief they stretched right out and did their work like a pair of fine little machines.

"You ought to be a horse dealer, Chief," I said, finally, when I saw that he wasn't going to talk about the evening. "You'd be able to double the price of any horse by the way you handle 'em. You really ought to be a horse dealer."

"I ought to be in hell!" he cried out suddenly. "And I *am* in hell!"

That took the breath and the gimp out of me. I sat without an idea, simply afraid of the future, all the way home. When we got there, I told him that I'd put the horses up. He simply said:

19

"You go to bed. I'll take care of them!"

I crawled out of the corral, and went through the swing gate into the yard, and pulled a furry leaf off the fig tree, and sat on the veranda and tried to think, and couldn't see a thing in the back of my mind except the smile of Allardyce and the sheen of her eyes.

Afterwards, the Chief came with his soft step and almost surprised me. We smoked cigarettes together in silence. Then he came over and put a hand on my shoulder and said:

"It's no good, Rickie. I know you want to help, but I can't talk to you about it."

He went in to bed, and I followed him, but I lay awake for a long time with the dread puckering my eyes and making my heart thump.

The next day, the first thing I heard was the Chief, singing. And that fair beat me! Yes, he was singing like a bird—if you can imagine a bird with a baritone voice as big as the bark of a mastiff.

We went out and rode range, and built fence together, and did a lot of other things. The Chief spoke never a word except about what we were doing, and about the kinks in a Roman-nosed devil of a roan horse that he was smoothing out in his spare time, just then. When we came in for lunch, who but Allardyce was there? She wasn't staying. She was hurrying home. But she had talked plenty to mother in the meantime. Mother had red eyes and was calling her "my dear."

Allardyce came up to me and gave me her hand.

"I hope you're going to like me," she said.

"Great Scott, Allardyce," said I, "what a fool I'd be if I didn't like you!"

The Chief walked out to the gate with her, to see her onto her horse. I went back into the house and persuaded my mother to come in with me, so that the two of them would be half private for a moment. Mother was still wiping eyes that wouldn't stay dry.

"Some day you're going to find a fine honest girl for yourself, Rickie," said she, giving me a thought.

"I'd rather find one with ten thousand head of cattle and plenty of rocks in the bank," said I.

She gave me half a look and half a smile, as though to reassure me that she knew I didn't mean it. But she couldn't pry her mind loose from her favorite son. Then the Chief came in, wearing a very sober face, though he made himself pleasant enough during lunch. Mother rattled on and on about Allardyce, and what a beauty she was, and what a good girl, and what a glorious girl, and what a darling, and all that. I saw that every word of praise that she said about Allardyce was sweet poison for the tooth of my brother.

Why?

Well, I didn't know. I didn't know anything about him, and when the dark and empty look came into his eyes again, it made me sick at heart. But what could I do or say? He knew that I wanted to help, and he had told me that there was nothing I could do.

The whole range knew that Allardyce and the Chief were to be married, and the whole range approved of that marriage, I think. People took it for granted that the Chief was really settling down. Of course Allardyce had all the money in the world. And what was there to keep them from making a success out of life?

Then, a couple of days after that, the first blow fell, suddenly, when we were going along as smoothly as water running downhill.

It was the arrival of Jim Ferrald, one evening after supper. Some one knocked at the front door; the Chief answered the call and failed to come back. Finally my mother grew worried, so I went out and found the two of them sitting in the moonlight on the edge of the veranda. The Chief started a little.

"This is Jim Ferrald, an old friend of mine," he said. "My brother Rickie, Jim."

Ferrald gave me a good long look, easing himself up from his place on the board, and gradually extending his hand. Of course I knew a good deal about him, because he had been one of the big names in the gang that

21

had followed the Chief. He looked like his dangerous reputation, too.

He was built long and narrow and round all the way. You could see that he was immensely strong in spite of his narrowness, and he had hands and feet big enough for two. Tradition said that he had killed more than one man with his naked hands, and I believed it when he gave me a grip.

He had a voice without any feeling in it, a hard, ringing, metal voice, as he said: "I'm sure glad to meet a brother of the Chief."

He was such a formidable-looking fellow that I was rather surprised to hear Ferrald calling my brother "Chief." You see, he used the word as though it were more than a nickname.

He stood there waiting to learn why I had come out. I muttered something about my mother and asked them to come into the house.

"We're talking, son; we're talking," said Ferrald, and with a wave of his hand he sort of brushed me away from the place.

I had a chance to see the Chief's face in the moonlight, though, and thought that it looked uncommon strained. So I did a pretty bad thing. I went back, reported to mother that everything was all right, and then sneaked into the front room, and listened as well as I could to the quiet of their voices on the veranda.

I got there just in time, too. I mean, just in time to hear Ferrald saying:

"If I thought that you'd let me down, Chief—if I thought that you wouldn't go on the trail with me to get the dirty skunks who killed Jerry—I'd try to murder *you*. And I mean it. I'm not threatening. I know what you can do with yourself. Only I mean that I've known all this time that it was more than *I* could wangle alone—to tackle Loomis—and now if you turned me down, I'd go crazy, I guess."

I patched the whole story up out of those words. The "Jerry" he spoke about was his brother—Jerry Ferrald

22

who had been with the Chief, too, and who had been killed in the last big job just before the Chief was captured. And every one said that it was the work of Harry Loomis, who had been jealous of the Chief's gang and had combined somehow with the officers of the law to smash the outfit.

I heard the Chief's soft voice answering:

"How could I turn you down, Jimmy?"

And when I understood what he said, my heart fairly stopped beating. Because of course it meant ruin for everything and everyone. It meant going on a blood trail, and that meant a killing on one side or the other, and that meant the iron hand of the law, again, and the smashing of all the hopes of happiness between the Chief and Allardyce Benchley.

CHAPTER IV

PRISON SHAKES

THE Chief brought Jim Ferrald into the house, after a time. The face of my mother was a study when she had to shake hands with that crook. But the Chief had invited him to spend the night with us.

That puzzled me. Nobody was more sensitive than the Chief to the feelings of others, and I was amazed to think that he would ask Ferrald to stay, or even that he would bring him in to see mother, because of course the mere mention of the name was enough to make her see all the dark side of the Chief's past. Mother set her teeth, managed a smile and a handshake, and then got out of the way. A little later, Ferrald went off to bed, and then the Chief stood up and stretched.

We were in the dining room. We had a parlor, too, but it never was used much. Usually we were too tired at the end of the day to do more than sit and chin over the coffee at the end of supper. Talk grows cold, if you go from one room into another.

"I'm turning in. Good night, Rickie," said the Chief.
I took my nerve in both hands and stood up to him.
"Wait a minute," said I.

"Oh, yes?" said he, pausing at the entrance to the narrow hall. He turned back to me, smiling, but in spite of the smile I could see the strain in his eyes.

I had scraped together a few words, and I used them now.

"This is pretty thick, Chief," I told him. "You can't bring fellows like Ferrald around mother."

"Oh, can't I?" said he.

"No, you can't."

He closed the door into the hall and came back to me. He leaned one hand on the edge of the table and faced me, and smiled at me.

"Go ahead, Rickie," said he.

I took a breath.

"After I met Ferrald," said I, "I sneaked inside and got into the front room. I heard part of what you said to him, and what he said to you."

"You did that?" said the Chief.

Suddenly he was a terrible thing to face. His voice had not altered. It was just in his eyes and his expression— as though he were ready to tear me to pieces. I could understand why men said that even better fighters than the Chief were never able to *face* him. All the strength went out of me. I shuddered, and said:

"I had to listen in. It was wrong. But I'm glad that I did it. I heard you tell Jim Ferrald that you'd go on the trail with him. You'd go after Loomis. And you can't go!"

"Can't I?" said he, and smiled. It was half a sneer, that smile, and it whipped hot blood all through me.

"You can't go," said I, "unless you're a dog! You can't let Allardyce go hang, and that's what it means if you start working with guns again. The law will be after you. You know that!"

I threw out a hand to him.

"Chief," I begged, "don't throw up the chance that you

24

have now! Don't let a wolf like Ferrald drag you into trouble."

He looked at me with a queer smile.

"Don't talk so loud," said he. "Ferrald might hear you. He might come out with a gun, and he's a bad fellow to handle."

I stared.

"He won't try to start anything with me while you're here," said I.

"He might," said the Chief, "and I wouldn't help you."

"You wouldn't?"

"No," said he.

I shut my eyes and tried to think back. My brother had such control of himself, his manners were always so amiable, that for all I knew, he might have been despising me, hating me for years. I could even imagine that he did, because a fellow with my mug and my way would be an anchor to hold him back from a better sort of people. But then I remembered ten thousand acts of kindness and gentleness, and I couldn't believe that he meant what he said—that he would chuck me in a pinch.

"You don't mean that," said I, opening my eyes and looking away from the past.

"I do mean it," said he.

He kept part of his smile, but I saw that he was chalky-white, and the horrible empty darkness was flowing out of his eyes.

"Chief," I groaned, "what do you mean to do? Are you really giving up Allardyce? Are you going back to the old life?"

"I'm not going back to the old life, but I'm giving up Allardyce," he told me. "I'm going away."

I looked at the whiteness of his face again.

"Why?" I asked.

"Because I'm afraid," said he.

I was handy to a chair, so I caught the back of it and lowered myself to the seat, always watching him.

"Afraid of what?" I asked.

"Ferrald," said he.

"It's not true, Chief!" I gasped at him. "Ferrald? You could eat ten men like him! He was only one of a crowd. You were head and shoulders above him, in the old days."

"These are new days," said the Chief.

I tried to speak. The words wouldn't come. I made a cigarette. My fingers tore it to pieces against my will. I made another and lighted it. The smoke had no taste.

"You mean what you say!" I said at last, still staring.

"Yes," said he.

I knew, now, what the darkness was that was in his eyes. It *was* fear, mixed up with despair and loneliness of the spirit; it was the look of a man who stands at the end of the world without a companion.

Fear? The Chief? I tried to put the two ideas together, but they wouldn't fit.

"Go on," I said. "If dying for you will help you, I'm ready to die, I guess. But go on. There's something that I ought to know."

He nodded. Now, to my death day I shall remember the pale stone of his face, and the horrible half smile on his lips, as he talked.

"I used to be the champion fat-head of the world," he said. "I used to be the hardest hombre, and the toughest fellow going. I thought I was. I thought I could be bent, but not broke. But I was wrong."

"What broke you?" I asked.

"The pen," said he. "I bucked them. I laughed at the rules. And they broke me."

He waited for the horrible thought to soak thoroughly into my mind. Then he went on:

"The assistant warden told me he'd do it. He said that he'd break me so that I'd get down on my knees and crawl to him and beg his pardon. And that was what I did, in the end. I got down on my knees—and I crawled."

I buried my face in my hands.

I heard him saying:

"I was sure of myself. I was sure that I could stand beatings, burnings, even. I could stand ten years of

26

bread and water, and still damn them to their faces. But they didn't use starving or floggings."

"Chief," I whispered, "what did they do to you?"

I got up and ran to him and gripped his arm, and then I felt a strange, electric shuddering of his flesh.

"They put me in the dark," said he.

I don't know why that ran a knife into me, but it did. For the darkness was what I had seen pouring out of his eyes, the empty darkness.

"They put me in solitary, in the dark," said he. "And they—"

His voice went all to pieces.

I walked over to the window and held onto the back of a chair, and kept facing the window, though I couldn't see anything outside.

"Afterwards," said the Chief, "I crawled, all right. I crawled—on my knees—up to the assistant warden—and asked his pardon. He kicked me in the face. He said that I was only a dog, and that he always knew how to handle dogs."

"I'm going to kill him," I said to the window.

"So I'm pulling out," said the Chief. "I thought for a day or two that perhaps I could slide through and have a chance at a happy life with Allardyce—but I was wrong— I was wrong—"

I don't want to talk about what he did then, or how he dropped into a chair, or how I heard him sobbing. Not the sobbing of a woman or a child, but the terrible weeping of a man whose soul is going to pieces. That was when I knew what it meant to see a "broken" man. They had broken him in the prison. I wanted to get the assistant warden of that place and kill him, little by little, making his life last a year, while I whittled his body away. There was nothing but murder in me.

I got some whisky. His hand was shuddering so that he could not hold the glass. I put it to his lips. His head was shuddering so that he could not drink. I had to take the crook of my arm around his neck and squeeze hard,

27

to steady him, and then I managed to pour the whisky down that frightful mouth.

I poured down two glasses. Then I went and sat at the table and made myself face him. I got hold of his hand, and gripped it, and he gripped back until the bones seemed to be smashing inside my flesh.

He got out a handkerchief and mopped his face.

"You could have slid out and gone away, and never have let me see this," said I. "But you wouldn't sneak out. You wanted to let me have something to tell Allardyce, some reason to give her. Chief, I love you more than ever! You're not going away. You're afraid that Ferrald will jump you unless you promise to go on the trail with him, but that won't happen. You're going to stay here—and I'm going to *kill* Ferrald!"

He looked up at me. The tears were gone from his eyes. His face was white stone, if you can imagine white stone with a quiver in it.

"I can't think," he said. "Wait a minute. It's the prison shakes. They hit a man, now and then. They've hit me this time. They'll hit me again—and again. Every time a crisis comes, a big moment, I'm going to pieces—like this!"

I swallowed, or tried to swallow. I made another cigarette, and gave it to him, and lighted it. I made one for myself. We smoked those two cigarettes out, never looking at one another. All the while I was building myself up for the great thing—I would kill Ferrald. I would have to kill him!

Then the voice of the Chief came to me—and it was his calm, usual voice. He was saying:

"You couldn't handle Ferrald. He's as good with guns as ever I was. He's better than I ever was, except that he thought that I was his master. There was nothing weak about him except the thinking!"

Suddenly I knew that the Chief was right. I could feel it in my bones—that Ferrald would crumple me up, and make nothing of the job.

CHAPTER V

THE FIRST PROBLEM

THE more I thought of Ferrald, the more certain I was
that the man was a devil. I said so. I said there must be
something that the law could do to stop him.

"Shall I give information against a man who used to
work with me, who used to ride with me?" said the Chief.
And his voice lifted a little, and rang a little. I felt his old
dominance come over me again. "Besides, according to
his lights, he's tackling the finest job he could do in the
world."

"A job of murder, eh?"

"He wants to revenge his brother. He knows that he
never could handle Loomis alone. Partly because Loomis
is a cunning devil, partly because Loomis has nothing but
superdevils around him. When Ferrald heard that I was
out of prison, he came to me like a homing pigeon, knowing that the Chief who used to lead him would never
turn him down in a pinch like this. I tried to argue him
out of it, to-night, but I couldn't do it. He's pinned his
faith to me. And if I failed him, he'd do what he says—
he'd try to tear the heart out of me, if he died during the
job.

"I've given you the facts, Rickie. There's nothing for
me to do except to slip away, to-night. I've got to get to
the other side of the world, put on a new name, grow a
beard and mustache, let my hair grow long, bury myself
in some sort of a beachcombing future."

All of this he said calmly, but while I heard him, I was
thinking of something else.

The first major difficulty was to get that Ferrald out of
the way, and a manner of doing that had popped into
my brain. I wasn't thinking far into the future, but just
around the corner of that first problem—how to get Ferrald out of the way. And I felt I'd reached a solution.

29

"Chief," I said, "a thousand times since I was a little kid, I've done what you've asked me to do, blind. Is that true?"

He nodded.

"Will *you* do one thing blind, for me?" I asked.

"What?" he asked.

"Go saddle a horse, leave the place, and not come back till to-morrow evening at the earliest?"

"And then?" asked the Chief.

"Don't ask me," said I. "Just go."

He shook his head.

"You mean to have it out with Ferrald," he said. "But that's no good. You don't know Ferrald. I do. He's a fighting maniac who never gets a clouded brain. He can shoot straight by instinct. His bullets hit the mark like homing pigeons. He could almost kill men around a corner. Are you following me, Rickie? And although he looks slender, he has the strength of rawhide."

I nodded.

"I won't try to touch him," said I. "I'm asking you to do something blind. Will you do it?"

He studied me for a time. Then he said: "I'll do it."

"Roll a blanket, and then start," said I.

He got up without another word of argument. Presently he came through the dining room again carrying his roll. I went out with him, saw him snake a rope over the head of a horse in the corral as easily as though the moonlight had been sunshine, and helped him saddle and bridle the mustang.

He shook hands with me. Suddenly I felt that he considered me a man for the first time, and that was about worth dying for, let me tell you! He said nothing; the tremor in his hand was more than words to me, though. And I finally watched him up the road until it turned him out of sight.

Then I went back to the house, undressed, went to bed, turned on my face—which I hadn't done since I was a kid—and went to sleep in ten seconds.

When I got up and dressed, I went into the kitchen,

said good morning to mother, and stood in front of her startled face for a moment.

"Where's my boy?" she asked me. "He didn't sleep in his bed last night!"

"He's in a safer place than home, just now," I told her. "Where's Jim Ferrald?"

Her face puckered with distaste, as she hooked her thumb toward the back porch. I left her staring after me, holding her biscuit cutter above the floury slab of white dough.

When I stepped onto the back veranda, Ferrald was there sitting in a chair tilted toward the wall.

"Where's the Chief?" he asked, by way of good morning.

"Gone," said I.

"Gone?" echoed Ferrald.

He stood up. His eyes flickered back and forth, from side to side, as though he expected danger to run at him from either hand.

"Gone, eh?" said he.

"Yes, gone," said I. "He wants things to start. I'm to ride on with you. He'll be back here and pick up the trail that you leave behind. You know how he rides. He'll overtake us in a day or two."

Ferrald pointed a forefinger into the thin air and stabbed at an idea.

"I'm to go on—with you. He's to pick up the trail afterwards. He's to rejoin us, eh? Then why the devil don't he come with us to start with?"

"How do I know?" said I. "I'm not such a fool as to try to be deeper than the Chief!"

His eyes flashed at me. His long, bony face twisted a little to one side.

"You talk hard, kid," said he. "How hard *are* you?"

"Hard enough to know a friend from an enemy," said I.

"And what am I to you, then?" he asked.

"A man who needs help," said I. "And I'm on the job."

"*You* are on the job?" said he.

I endured his faint sneer as well as I could.

31

"Not that I care about you," I told him, "but because the Chief wants me to line out with you. We're to get to the right country and open up the skirmishing and find out how the land lies. Then he'll come on."

Suddenly a flash of a different sort came into the eyes of Ferrald, and half of the suspicion left his face.

"That sounds like the old Chief," he said, grinning. "We make the opening for the wedge, and then there's to be a chance that he'll come up with more men, and smash them up. Only why didn't he tell me what was in his mind before he left, last night?"

"How do I know?" I asked. "Except that you were asleep and snoring—besides, I suppose he thought that you'd do as he said, without arguing."

"Yeah, I snored, all right," agreed Ferrald. He seemed to be convinced that all was well by small details like this. "And he sends his own brother along with me," he continued, arguing with himself, out loud. "That shows that he's with me, lock, stock, and barrel."

"With you?" said I. "Did the Chief ever turn a friend down?"

Jim Ferrald struck his fist into the palm of his right hand.

"No," he said. "He never did!"

"He never could," said I.

"No," said Ferrald. "He never could. Am I to leave word with your ma where we're riding?"

"Tell me, and I'll leave a note for him," I answered, shuddering a little at the thought of my mother being let into this secret.

"Anything you say, doctor," remarked Ferrald. "We'll head right up for Culver Peak, and we'll be found easy, somewhere along Culver Canyon."

"I'll write it down," I told him.

I went into the house as though to write the note, but what I actually scribbled was:

DEAR CHIEF: I'm off on a ride. Don't try to follow.

You're not wanted in this business at all. God bless you and good luck to you.

Adios,   RICKIE.

I sealed that in an envelope, and put it on the table in his room. Then I went back to warn Ferrald.

"Don't say a word to my mother," I said to him. "We'll simply tell her that we've gone out to try to shoot a deer."

"Why, sure, kid, sure!" agreed Ferrald, growing more amiable all the time. "I know what women are. I was married to a long-faced squaw of a Canuck female, once, and I found out that the only way to get along with women is to lie to 'em regular."

"And when they find out?" I asked.

"Why, then they feel so bright and superior that they forgive you right away," said Jim Ferrald.

CHAPTER VI

RIDING TO TROUBLE

I'VE always thought my mother guessed at something, when I remarked during breakfast that I could show Ferrald some good deer shooting, and when he accepted before the suggestion was an invitation. We would start out right after breakfast and try our luck, we agreed. When my mother heard this plan formulated, she looked down at the table and picked a piece of toast to bits, in silence, though as a rule she generally protested against hunting as a waste of time, lead and patience.

This very silence of hers bothered me a good deal. She had no comments to make while Ferrald and I saddled up. But when we rode out the corral gate and headed across country, I saw her standing on the veranda, shading her eyes so that she could follow us to the last. It gave me a queer feeling. When she had dwindled to a mere streak of shadow, wavering with distance, the thought of her was a stronger and a deeper feeling than it had ever been before.

I felt lonely. The most comfortable place in the world appeared to be the kitchen where she would soon be working. And I thought of how she would wait for us to appear for supper—for us, and for the Chief. And how she would stand out by the front fence and look up and down the road until thick darkness. And how she would afterwards sit on the veranda wrapped in a shawl and go to sleep there. But perhaps she would never lay eyes on me again; perhaps she would have only a cold comfort out of the coming of the Chief late in the night.

I always thought that my mother was a rather dull woman, given to nagging, but when I turned in the saddle and gave the last look toward her, I felt as weak and lonely as a child in the dark.

Ferrald was watching me with a cross between a grin and a sneer.

"Feeling kind of sick, kid?" he asked me.

I looked straight back at him. It made me mad to have him talk like this, but I decided that I would be honest, so I simply said:

"Yeah, I'm homesick before I'm out of sight of the old place."

Ferrald laughed. "That's all right," he said. "At your age, I would have felt the same way. If you've got the nerve to admit you're afraid, you'll soon get over it. How much help would you be in a gun fight?"

"I'm not lightning flash," I said, "and I can't hit a dime at twenty-five yards with a revolver."

"Who can, unless he takes a target pistol and a half minute for drawing a bead?" answered Ferrald. "But take and throw some lead into that tree, yonder."

He twisted and pointed back toward a tree which we had just passed and which was about twenty yards or so behind. I knew what he wanted, the minute he spoke— fast, hard shooting, no matter whether I hit the target or not. So I slashed the Colt out from under the pit of my left arm and fanned the five shots in it at that tree trunk.

34

It seemed to me that the gun was jumping crazy in my hand, but when we went back to look, there were two slugs in that trunk, about four feet from the ground. The trunk was about the size of a man's body, I should say.

Ferrald rode on with me, and while I loaded up the gun again, he said:

"That's all right. It ain't the kind of shooting that will make a gent famous, but it's the kind that'll be useful in a real brawl."

"I'm not real good," said I. "I've seen the Chief knock quarters out of the air, and nickels, too."

"I've seen him do that, and he's seen me manage the same thing," said Ferrald. "I can shoot as straight as he ever could, but I'm a shade slower and I'm not quite so steady in a pinch. The difference is mainly that he loves a fight when it's going on, and all I like is the results after it's over."

He added, after a minute: "I've heard him singing through the roar of the guns, kid. That's what I've heard him do!" Ferrald canted his head to the side and shook it a little, in his admiration and his wonder.

I could see that to him the Chief was a god on earth, a superman. And then I thought of the poor, trembling, broken wreck who had sat at the table with me the night before and I went sick and cold again.

Take it all in all, I wanted a little more time than we had before us, on this ride. I wanted a couple of days, say, during which I could get used to the idea of the trouble that lay ahead. But it was going to be too short. We were passing through the foothills of the Blue Water Mountains already, and we'd be up around Culver Canyon sometime in the afternoon. Almost any minute after the middle of the day, trouble was apt to come jumping at us, because if Ferrald was out hunting for Loomis, I could be pretty sure that Loomis and his gang of crooks would be looking for Ferrald.

I asked Ferrald about that, and he gave me his sour smile. It seemed to hurt his face.

"You're right," he said, "Loomis knows that I'm after

35

him. And he'll have his thugs on the lookout for me. Oh, there's been some long riding done, the last week or so, since I met up with Joe Toole in the town of Blue Water!"

"What did you do to Toole?" I asked.

"Me? What did I do? Why, I shot the devil out of him, was what I did," said Ferrald. He kept on smiling speaking slowly, tasting the scene over again as he talked about it.

"This here Toole was one of the gang that jumped my brother Jerry," said Ferrald. "They got in from behind, too. The dirty rats! The dirty low, sneakin' rats! Oh, they wouldn't never 'a' dared to look him in the face, no more than they would 'a' dared to look the Chief in the face. But they got him from behind, and he went down, fightin' men he couldn't see. And when I bumped into this here Toole, he was standin' in the post office at Blue Water readin' a letter from his girl, by the fool look on his face. I says to him: 'Hullo, Joe. Here's a present from me.'

"He spun around and give me a look. I can still see him, and the green in his face. I had a gun out.

" 'Fill your hand, you,' said I.

" 'Jimmy,' said Toole, 'it wasn't me that plugged Jerry. I swear that I didn't have nothing at all to do with—'

" 'Fill your hand!' said I.

"He filled his hand, all right. And there was a funny thing happened, along about then," said Ferrald. "You'd 'a' laughed if you'd seen it. I mean, you'd 'a' busted yourself, if you'd seen Toole reach for his gun and start hollering for help, at the same time. I mean, him being a grown-up man, and hollering for help. I had to laugh, kid. I started in laughing so's I could hardly shoot straight. A grown-up man like Toole, that had murdered Jerry, and standing there and hollering for help while he makes his draw. I plastered him right between the eyes, and that stopped his yelling, all right.

"Well, when I rode out of that town of Blue Water, I knew that all of the Loomis boys would pretty soon

36

have the good word that I was around that part of the country, and they'd get ready for me. They'd know that the Chief was out of jail, too, and they'd guess that him and me was goin' to come up there and raise a little trouble."

"But look here," I said, gaping at this murderer a little. "Look here, Jim—why show your hand to the crooks you're going to try to hunt down? Why tip your hand that way? Is that any good? You throw away all your chance of taking them by surprise."

"What's the good of taking them by surprise?" said Jim Ferrald. "You ain't doing a man no harm if you kill him when he ain't looking. You're just doing him a favor. It ain't the shot of electricity that hurts the birds in the chair—it's the preparations, the putting on the bandages, and the blindfold cap, and the lashing of the legs and the arms, and everything like that. That's what makes it hell. And that's what some of the Loomis crew is going through. They're getting ready for me and the Chief. They know that we'll come. They sure know that I only waited for the Chief to turn up, and then that I'd come. So I left them Toole for a calling card, and then I come down here, to let 'em stew in their own juice, and wait for me to come back."

He began to laugh, after he had said that. This laughter was the one thing in the world that was uglier than his smile. I mean, he had a way of wabbling his shoulders up and down, while his chin poked in and out, so that he looked like a buzzard swallowing a bone.

"Maybe even Loomis is a little scared!" said he. "Not of me, mind you, but knowing that the Chief will soon be on the trail."

I squinted and took in a breath, thinking of how long, long it would be before ever the Chief got on a trail like this. I thought of another thing, too—of what would happen when Ferrald found out that the Chief was not coming near to help! He'd murder me first, and then he'd go back and murder the Chief. And when the Chief saw him coming—he'd get down and crawl! I saw all of those

37

pictures, and it was a pretty seasick feeling, let me tell you!

Then I began to wonder what sort of a man it was whose murder had broken up Jim Ferrald so much.

I said to him: "Look here—tell me about Jerry, will you?"

"Jerry?" said he, quick as a flash. "Ain't the Chief told you about Jerry?"

"Sure," I said. "But I'd like to hear what you say."

"Well," said Ferrald, "Jerry was the best partner, and the squarest shooter, and the most amusin' sort of a gent to have around that you ever seen in your life. He was *right,* is what he was."

"How did he come to get into the Chief's game?" I asked. "Did you fetch him into the long riding?"

Jim Ferrald laughed.

"No, sir. Other way round," he explained. "Jerry was likely to get cantankerous when he played poker. He didn't mind hardly anything, but he hated to lose at poker. And he got into a game, one day, and he began to lose. And the first thing you know, he started to mark the cards. He was slick, that way. You never seen anybody smarter than Jerry was. And pretty soon he'd won back his money and some more with it, and then an hombre at the table, he takes up the pack of cards and looks hard at the backs of the cards, and bawls out that Jerry is a crook. Just a plain, ordinary fool, that hombre was, and makes a grab for a gun, and Jerry drops him.

"Well, there was a commotion, and Jerry got away with no more'n a couple of flesh wounds, and rides up into the mountains. And when he don't come home, I go up after him, and I see the Chief, and I decide to stay on, myself. That's how it come about.

"Jerry, he takes me to see the Chief, and the Chief makes a talk to me and says that they're living outside the law and they're working together for a free life, and each gent is helping his partners. There's to be no fighting inside the gang, and there's to be no murder outside of it. There's to be no horse stealing or such, and every man pays for what he gets when he's riding on duty and needs grub or anything else. There's to be no bullying of sheep-herders, even, and if the squatters charge three prices for everything, they're just to be paid, and no argument. That's how the Chief built up his reputation. There's a thousand gents up there in the mountains ready to die for him, still, because he never did no harm. All he ever nicked was the big gents, the big operators that had so many millions they could afford to lose a few thousands, here and there!"

I liked what he said about the Chief, but I began to wonder a little what sort of a fellow his brother had been, the one who hated to lose at cards, and cheated to win, and covered his cheating with murder!

"Tell me some more about Jerry!" said I.

"Sure. I could talk all day and all night about him," said Jimmy Ferrald. "He was a funny bird, Jerry was. He never took no stock in women, Jerry didn't. He was like me, that way. But the way he done was funny. You'd 'a' laughed. When he had some time off and a pile of cash, he'd go and find him a pretty girl and spend a lot of money on her, and give her a whirl. He didn't look like me, none. He was something worth seeing, Jerry was, and dog-gone me, before you knew it, he'd be engaged to the girl, and go around and have a fine time with her, and about the week before the wedding day, he'd just step out of the picture and leave her behind to twiddle her thumbs!"

This picture pleased Jimmy Ferrald such a lot that he almost fell off his horse, he laughed so hard. I tried to smile, too, but the smile went sour on me.

"He was always up to something," said Jimmy. "Even when he was a kid. There was a schoolteacher that didn't like Jerry, and Jerry laid for him one winter night, when it was about zero, and roped him, and tied him up to a tree, and left him there. And when they found him the next morning, he was blue as a stone. He got pneumonia and pretty near died. You would a laughed to see how close that teacher come to passing out! But Jerry

39

was like that. If he got a grudge agin' you, he'd take it out on you, one way or another. Yeah, he could be poison, when he wanted to be. Like the time he found Turk Wilder in a saloon in Phoenix and shook hands like he was glad to see Wilder, and then pulled Turk's own gun and shot him dead with it.

"I tell you what, it was a treat to listen to Jerry talk, because he had something to *talk* about. Some folks got kind of mean because Jerry wouldn't lift a hand around camp. He was always a great hand to develop rheumatism, or a fever, or something like that, when he was in camp, and lie around and get himself waited on. But I never minded none doing his share of the chores besides my own, because it was a real treat to have Jerry lie around and yarn and drink coffee, after he'd had his fill of eats!"

Here Jimmy Ferrald made a pause, and said again: "Take him by and large, he was about the best partner and the best company that I ever seen in my life!"

I had enough of Jerry Ferrald, by that time, because for all that I could see, the Loomis crew had done a good job when they bumped him off. But I'd started his brother on a topic that he loved, and he wouldn't let go of it, but kept hammering away all day long. Nothing that Jerry had done seemed really wrong to Jim, though it began to leak out that Jim himself was a decent enough sort, in same ways. He was simply one of those people who think that life is no more sacred than dollars, but he was certainly not the sort to cheat at cards or murder a man while shaking hands with him, or let down a partner in any way.

We were getting up into the mountains, that afternoon, and heading toward Culver Canyon, and watching the big Blue Waters walk higher and higher into the sky. It was a good country, with plenty of water running everywhere, and fine open slopes for grazing cattle, and plenty of cracking big trees, and deer in the valleys and mountain sheep in the uplands, and about everything that a man could wish to have, to say nothing of the white summits that stuck into the blue of the sky, here and there.

But for my part, I could only think about Loomis and his gang and the trouble that was lying ahead. All the beauty went out of the mountains and the valleys. The creek waters had no sparkle for me, and when we looked down some long slope at the blue of one of the glacial lakes that had given the mountains their name, my eye was never pleased. I had a cemetery feeling all the time. Then we had our first look at a human being since leaving home.

CHAPTER VII

SUSAN CARR

WE were coming through a grove of second-growth trees when Ferrald spotted the rider and jerked his mustang to a halt. I pulled up mine, also, a little ahead of him, so that I was near the verge of the trees and could see better what was going on outside.

The rider was a girl, who came zooming over the top of a hill and walloping down the green of the slope with a little sleek-skinned dog yelping and racing behind her. She could ride, that girl could. She rode so well that all I looked at was the horse and the way she rode it, at first. It was a black mare, small, with the legs of a deer, and a fierce look, and a proud head, and it showed its independence after a second or two, by beginning to pitch at the sight of a white rock, and it was beautiful to see the way that girl straightened the mare out with her spurs and her quirt.

They were a real pair of aces, that horse and that girl. They fitted each other. They were out of the same pack of cards. By thunder, she was a pretty little Indian! I mean, she was as dark as an Indian, but no Indian ever had a face like that! no Indian could ever laugh like that; no Indian ever had eyes like that.

41

She went scooting over the edge of the hill. She seemed to be galloping right off into the sky, and as she dropped out of sight, the little sleek midget of a brown dog found a hole in the ground and shoved its nose into it, and began to yelp and bark and try to dig its way down to the trouble that was inside.

Then one of those things happened that make you feel that you're all alone in the heart of the wilderness. A shadow slid like lightning over the bright grass of that hillside, there was a booming sound of wings exploding, and up into the air on a long slant sailed a bald eagle with that screeching little dog in its talons!

I got my horse out of the wood as fast as spurs could make it jump. The eagle was already over the edge of the hill. I heard the girl scream in the distance, and the bald-headed devil turned on a dime and came rushing back, climbing every instant. He wasn't very high up, though, and I got him with the first bullet I fired.

That .45 caliber slug made the feathers fly, I can tell you. The eagle staggered in the air, as though all the sense had gone out of his wings. Down he came, and forgot to drop the weight of the dog until he was close to the ground. The pup fell, rolled head over heels, jumped up, tucked its tail between its legs, and beat it for the skyline as fast as it could go.

The eagle, swinging low, whanged into a rock as though he were blind and then fell in a heap, dead as a doornail.

On top of this fast action, I heard the voice of Ferrald calling:

"Get hold of that girl and pump her for everything she knows. One man is better than two with a woman. You're alone. I'll foller on. Pump her, kid!"

Soon after that, the girl came soaring over the top of the hill with the little dog in her arms. She came sashaying right up to me, hopped out of the saddle, tucked her dog under her left arm, and gave me her hand.

Well, she wasn't big, but she was big enough. She

looked like she was a little too small, but when you sized her up, you could see that she was just right. There was a shine about her. It wasn't the brightness of her smile and her eyes, or the smooth of her skin—it was just a shine that was as much a part of her as breathing. She stood there and shone at me, I tell you, till I had to look down to the trail of the eagle's blood that had dripped across the grass. Maybe that should have been a signal to me that there was trouble ahead, but I was too bursting with happiness to think forward, just then.

"You can *shoot!*" she said to me.

"He was coming over pretty low down," I told her. "And you'd turned him, when you yelled out. Anyway, it was lucky. Is the dog hurt much?"

"Poor Snooky!" said the girl. "Look!"

Snooky was trying to squirm deeper under her arm, but she made him come out into the light again for a minute, and I could see that the talons had only given him three or four deep scratches.

"He's only eight months old," said the girl. "I wonder if it will break his spirit, or anything like that? Poor Snooky!"

She looked up at me again, smiling, making small of the thing, but with real trouble in her eyes. And right then and there I loved her. Something went into me, between the ribs, deeper than a knife.

She seemed to forget the dog, except with her hands. She stared at me, and I stared at her. And more than ever I wished anything in the world, I wished then for a different mug to show to her. I wanted to say: "I'm no wonder, but I'm not such a tramp as I look!"

All I did was to blurt out: "Who are you?"

"Susan Carr," said she. "Who are you?"

"Richard—Willis," said I.

For I knew, suddenly, that it was not for me to tell people that I wore the same name that belonged to the Chief—not up in the Blue Water Mountains, not even to this girl, in the region where Loomis was king.

"You plastered that eagle, Richard," said she.

She went over and looked down at the bird. The puppy began to squeal and wriggle in her arm. She leaned down and took hold of the tip of a wing, and spread it. And the sun shone through the feathers.

"Look!" said she.

I looked, all right. I knew what she meant—something about how that bird had been a king up in the blue, a few minutes before. But she didn't try to put the idea into words. She left half of it for me to guess at, and all at once that made me feel happy and at ease and sure of myself. I even forgot all about my ugly mug.

"He stubbed his toe on some bad luck, was all," said I. She dropped the wing.

"Riding through?" she said.

"Yeah. Hunting a job," I told her.

"A job?" said she. "Lumber? Mining? Wrangling horses? What?"

"I know cows pretty well," I told her. "I'm a fair sort of an average hand."

She looked me over. Her eyes went hard suddenly.

"Where do you pack your gun?" she asked. "That *was* a revolver I heard, wasn't it?"

I pulled the Colt from the spring holster. She took it and looked it over. She rubbed her thumb over the place where the sight had been filed off. She touched the spot where the trigger should have been. Then she gave the gun back to me, and frowned.

"You don't shoot straight by accident," said she.

"What are you driving at?" said I.

"You're one of the fellows who *have* to shoot straight. Is that the way of it?"

"Hold on," said I. "Because I've got a doctored gun, that doesn't mean that I'm a gunman, if that's what you're getting at."

"Humph!" says she. "No; you're just a poor little boy out in the big world, eh?"

I put the gun back under my arm and felt the fingers of the spring holster take hold of the weight of it, and I scowled back at her.

44

"Look," said I. "Don't go around reading minds. You might be wrong, sometimes."

"Yeah. Sometimes," said she.

She was hard-boiled. I could see that, and I was sorry about it. There was no woman in her eyes, now, as she looked me over. She was just like a man and a distant, cold, critical man. I could feel her glance going through me, but something told me that I should not argue, and I kept my mouth shut.

"Well," said Susan Carr, "do you really want a job?"

"I could use a job," said I.

"I mean, a real job. Not just a week on the place, but a job that you could stick to."

She was so straight and so direct that all at once I couldn't lie to her.

I got red. I could feel the heat burn up over my cheek bones and make my eyes fairly sting.

"No," I said, "I don't want a long job, I guess."

I kept my eyes right on her, and got redder and redder. I felt pretty bad, because I knew what she'd think—that I was some gunman that had got into trouble, and was up here in the hole-in-the-wall country to keep out of harm's way, for a time.

This girl, after a while, sighed a little. Then she laughed. She came right up and put her hand on my arm.

"All right, Dick," said she, dropping the Richard just like that, "I'll get you the job, if you want it. Come along home with me, and I'll make father take you on. Maybe you're not half as bad as you think you are. Anyway, it's hard for you to lie, isn't it?"

I got on my horse and rode right off with her. I tell you, I'd forgotten all about Ferrald. I didn't want to think back. Everything in life pointed forward, for me, and my mind went out into a gaudy future with every step that the horses took across the mountainside.

CHAPTER VIII

AN ODD JOB

I WON'T waste time talking about that ride, or telling how the sky was bluer than it ever had been before, and the sun more golden, and the grass a better green; but the one thing certain was that at least half of the world was wrapped up in this girl on the dancing black mare.

She called the horse Zigzag, from its nervous way of going, and that name shortened up to either Zig or Zag. It seemed to me a remarkable name for a remarkable horse; but everything connected with Susan Carr was remarkable, in my eyes. She was the sort of a girl, I could see at once, that you'd want to have around any old time, from beside an open fire in winter up to a bear hunt in the autumn. Anything that any other girl could do, she would do a little better, because there was not a shadow of fear in her eyes.

To look at her, and know how she must be a bullet through the brain of almost any man, was enough to make me despair. That was why I was sad and happy in one. And even a man like the Chief, except that he'd found a stylish Allardyce for himself, would have been knocked pretty dizzy by a look at Sue Carr.

Well, we cut along across the table-land, and through a winding ravine, and came out on the side of one of the lakes that give the Blue Water Mountains their name. By the color of it, you could tell that it was as deep as the sky, and had its roots down by the roots of the mountains. The pine trees marched down the side of the northern mountain and stood in a huge row at the edge of the water, looking at themselves; and down the southern mountain there was a sweep of grass over terraces, with only a tree here and there. On the whole, it was a mighty prosperous-looking valley, with a rambling old log house planted between the pine forest and the grasslands, just where a brook came shining into the lake.

"That's your home!" I said.

"How do you guess that?" asked the girl.

I started to say that it looked like her, which would have been a fool remark. Then I wanted to say that the blue of the lake and the beauty of the whole valley was just the sort of a land to hold a life like hers; but that sounded too fancy, so I wound up by saying nothing at all. And that made a greater fool of me than ever.

By the time I got through wondering what to say, and finding nothing, she was watching me out of the corner of her eye with just a glimmer of amusement.

Well, when we got near to the place, a pack of about twenty dogs came rushing out. There was hardly a clean-bred dog in that pack. Some of them looked like a cross between wolves and mastiffs; some looked half Airedale and half greyhound; some looked only like themselves, and nothing else in the world; but every last one of the lot was a fighting dog that you'd hate to meet in the dark, I can tell you. They came and jumped up around my horse as high as the pommel of the saddle. I took my quirt by the lash to have the loaded butt of it ready in case one of the brutes sank teeth in me, but the girl yelled at the pack and scattered it. They were such a vicious lot that, though they knew her, some of them went off snarling and looking back.

"What d'you feed them?" I asked her. "Indians and hobos?"

"Any meat that's red and raw," said the girl, and she looked at me with that glint in her eye again.

I could see that she wasn't taking me very seriously, but I was already nervous about a good many things. So far as I knew, that big old log house might be head-quarters for the entire Loomis gang, for we were pretty well into the heart of the Blue Waters, by this time.

A big Negress came out of the back door of the house as we drew near. She threw a dishpan of suds out onto the ground, and scattered a lot of chickens that were scratching around. And a gray pig came and gobbled up some bits of food that were left.

"Father home, Aunt Lizzie?" sang out the girl.

"I dunno," said Aunt Lizzie. "He's settin' out in front, but where his thoughts is, I dunno. What you been finding now, to drag home with you-all?"

The girl got down and showed Aunt Lizzie the cuts on the body of Snooky, and the big cook said:

"There ain't no luck ever comes out of first meetings that leaves blood on your hands!"

That struck me, at the time. It struck me a lot harder, later on. I've thought of it a thousand times since.

There was a corral as big as a field with good grass growing in it, and I turned the two horses into it after I had unsaddled them. The girl had asked me to stay the night in the house, because the sun was turning red in the west, by this time.

I carried the saddles and bridles around to the front of the house. There I found a huge whale of a man lying out in a canvas chair with his legs spread and his face turned toward the last heat of the sun. He was a tremendous man. His face and his hands were brown black from weathering. He had a big gray, pointed beard and a mustache that stuck straight out to the sides like an old-time Spaniard's. And his long gray hair fell down to his shoulders, nearly, and curled up a good bit at the end. His clothes were half worn out. The rowels of his spurs were as big as the palm of my hand. He looked lazy, but strong enough to lift a horse.

"That's my father. You may have heard of Ralph Carr?" said Susan.

I hadn't heard of him, but I knew that I'd never forget him.

"Father, this is Richard Willis," said Susan. "An eagle grabbed Snooky and sailed off with him, and Mr. Willis dropped that eagle with a snap shot—a revolver shot. It seems that he's looking for a job—more or less a temporary one. I thought you might fix him up."

All the while she was talking, Ralph Carr was gradually

48

opening his eyes. He didn't sit up, at the finish. He just extended his hand toward me. I took hold of it. It was as big as a ham, and a lot harder. Ralph Carr could have smashed me with one grip of that hand, I was sure.

"Eagles die pretty easy," he said. "The hawks are the tough devils, eh? I've seen a duck hawk hunt a bald-headed eagle right straight across the sky, swooping at the big fellow, and bouncing up into the blue again, and every time the eagle would flip over on its back and wait with its talons ready for a stroke, and every time that falcon would sheer off and slide back to the middle of the sky again. No, sir; there's more fight in a two-pound hawk than in all the big, hulking eagles that ever killed baby lambs. Sit down, Willis. Sue, bring us some whisky."

I thought this was a little odd as a speech of intro-duction, but Sue went off to get the whisky, first giving me a faint smile, as though to tell me that I must take care of myself with this strange character.

Mr. Carr had closed his eyes again, as he asked:

"What sort of work do you want?"

I told him that I could do most sorts of ranch work.

"I need somebody to do that work," said Carr. "I've got several thousand head of beef wandering around through these mountains, but I never can find a cow-puncher who's able to take the right sort of care of them. If the cow-puncher rides herd too closely, he gets a slug of lead through his head, one day. And then I have to bury him. And if he isn't fighting, I know that he's thrown in with the outlaws that live in this part of the world. Are you one of them?"

"No, I'm not one of them," said I.

"Too bad," answered Carr. "I have a lot of good friends among those boys."

"They shoot your cow-punchers and rustle your cows, and still they're your friends?" said I.

"I take people as I find 'em," answered Carr. "Never believe gossip and rumor. I've never seen any of my outlaw friends shoot any of my cow-punchers, and I've

49

never seen them rustle any of my beef. I'm not up that late at night. But if you want a job riding herd on my steers, you're welcome to it. I'll pay you whatever you think is right, and you can fix up your own hours. Jus' suit yourself."

I wonder if any other fellow ever had a job offered to him under conditions like that? I could name my own wages, and my own hours, and my job was to ride herd on cattle that were scattered all over the mountains, with nothing to do but dodge a few chunks of lead, from time to time, unless I came to terms with the outlaws who slaughtered those cows as they needed them or, perhaps, drove them off to sell at outside markets. The whole thing was pretty absurd. I couldn't tell what to say, but finally I said, "Yes."

Carr yawned. I had a glimpse of a mouth as red as the mouth of a wolf, and teeth as shining and white.

"That's settled, then," said he.

The girl came back, just then, carrying a small stone jug and a pair of glasses. I poured out the drinks. Carr took a brimming bumper. I took one finger, because I felt that I had to have my wits about me, in this place.

"Willis is going to take a job working my cattle," said Carr to his daughter. And between the words—I don't know exactly how or where—he made that glass of whisky disappear down his throat with a single gulp, hardly interrupting his flow of speech.

Susan Carr asked: "Why do you want to feed him to the wolves, father?"

"Every man to his own choice," answered Carr. "He knows the troubles and the dangers of the job. He won't take it unless he wants it."

A rider came in view, just then, jogging his horse around the edge of the lake. When he was close, the girl said:

"Father, that's Mr. McLintock, from Blue Water."

"Who's McLintock?" asked Carr, closing his eyes again and folding his immense hands over his stomach.

50

"He runs the general-merchandise store," said the girl. "And he's probably come up here to collect his bill."

"Has he?" said Carr, and yawned again, with opening his eyes or moving.

"Shall I get out of here?" I asked the girl quietly.

She looked at me with a shade of trouble in her face.

"No," she said, shaking her head. "It doesn't matter. Everybody knows that we owe money—tons of it—everybody knows that we never pay our bills!"

Her mouth twisted. I could see that it was poison to her, but she would not back down or criticize her father. She seemed to be challenging me to dare to think a single bad thought about the giant. For that matter, I didn't feel hostile toward him. In spite of the fact that he was enormous and she was small, there was a resemblance between them. And while she seemed to be always on fire, I suspected that now and then Carr himself could be kindled to a blaze, and that it might be a regular forest fire.

Mr. McLintock came up, now, and got off his horse. He was a man of fifty, iron-gray, with an eye that never left its mark. He walked straight up to Carr. He didn't lift his old felt hat in honor of the girl, and he gave her only a short nod.

"Mr. Carr," he said, "I've come up here from Blue Water because you didn't drop in yesterday to pay that bill. You promised me a month ago that you'd be in yesterday to pay that bill, and you didn't come. That's why I'm here!"

"Are you?" said Carr, just lifting the heavy lids of his eyes a fraction of an inch.

"Yes, I'm here, and I want my money," said McLintock.

"How much is the bill?" asked Carr.

"You stave me off, and stave me off, and promise, and delay," said McLintock, quietly raging, "and yet you don't even know the amount of the bill you owe me?"

"So it seems," said Carr.

51

"You owe me," said McLintock, "three hundred and forty-eight dollars and some odd cents."

"How odd are the cents?" said Carr.

"Are you going to try to make a fool out of me?" demanded McLintock.

"No, McLintock. You're not a fool," said Carr. "But why do you come up here? I haven't the money, or I would have sent it to you, I suppose. No use wasting your time to come up here!"

McLintock made a step forward, not to get nearer but simply to brace himself for his next speech. Then he said slowly, loudly, like a man who means every word and has weighed it beforehand:

"I'm not the only man you owe money to, Mr. Carr. I've talked with some of the other merchants in Blue Water. And, unless you do something to pay your debts, we're going to take action."

"Are you?" said Carr. "I don't blame you. Why don't you round up enough of my cattle to pay the bill, and let it go at that?"

"My bills ain't paid in kind; they're paid in cash!" said McLintock. "I'm no cowboy, neither. And, besides, it's as much as a man's life is worth to try to get hold of any of those cattle, because the valleys are full of the crooks of Loomis, and you know it. I ain't here to talk about cows. I'm here to talk about cash."

"How much cash?" said a new voice.

I turned about with a jerk. Three steps from me was a man I hadn't seen before, and how he'd got there I couldn't imagine. He was a slender fellow in loose clothes, and he stood in a slouch, but it was the slouch of a cat. The desert had made him, not the mountains, it seemed. His eyebrows and eyelashes and the hair beneath his old sombrero were all sun-faded. His eyes were set back in his head, with the sun wrinkles at the corners of them so that he always seemed to be narrowing his glance. He wore time-faded clothes, and his skin, even, was more gray than brown. He could have faded

52

into a desert setting as easily as any wolf. His voice was quiet, but it commanded attention well enough.

McLintock had whirled around with a grunt, for the stranger was standing just behind him. He glowered and demanded:

"Who are you?"

"I'm asking the size of the bill," said the stranger.

"Three hundred and forty-eight dollars, and what business is it of yours?" demanded McLintock.

The stranger held out a little wad of bills.

"Here's three hundred and fifty," said he. "The change will go as interest."

McLintock slowly moved out his hand, then took the money with a sudden decision.

"All right," he said. "Who are you, partner?"

"Father!" the girl had exclaimed to Carr. "Are you going to let him pay your bills?"

"Why not?" asked Carr. "There's enough beef on the range to pay him back. Good-by, McLintock."

The storekeeper made a little speech about the necessity of collecting old bills, and about regretting to trouble old patrons. Then he got onto his horse and rode back down the side of the lake with the shadow of his horse and himself moving across the sunset red on the water.

I gave him one glance and then stole a look at the girl. She was as stiff as a board with shame and anger. I decided that it was better to look at the stranger than at her. It was easier.

CHAPTER IX

HARRY LOOMIS

CARR did the next talking, rolling his head a little to the side so that he was facing the stranger more easily.

"Here's a lad that's just taken a job riding herd for

me, Harry," he said. "But wouldn't he do a lot better to get a job with you?"

"Perhaps," said the gray man.

He looked at me. I felt that I had never been noticed before by anybody in the world. No one else had the eyes to see through the flesh to the spinal marrow, this way.

"I'm going to pay back that money to you, Harry!" said the girl. "If father has no shame—"

"Sue," said the father. "Do I have to send you to the house?"

She turned about and stared at him, and he looked back at her from under the heavy lids of his eyes. After a moment, she went over to his chair and stood behind it, her elbows resting on the top of it, and her eyes fixed on her father's head. It was a strange thing. I felt that there was a great bond between the two of them, I could hardly say how powerful. But suddenly I respected them both a great deal more than before.

"Your father knows that the money's nothing," said the stranger. "Is this young man a friend of yours, Sue?"

"He's too good a friend," she answered, "for me to want him to work for you. But that seems to be what he's trained for."

"What makes you think so?" asked he.

"Well, I saw him shoot an eagle out of the air," she returned.

The stranger had never moved his eyes from me during this time. Now he asked: "Do you know me?"

"No," said I.

"I'm Harry Loomis," he told me. "Do you want to work for me? Think you'd like it?"

From the first moment I saw him, I had been bracing myself for some sort of a shock, because the air of the place seemed to have changed. Because I was braced, I was able to stand the surprise, just now. But the shock turned me as light and cold as a leaf on a tree. I could have blown away in a puff of wind, when I realized that I was standing in front of the great Loomis himself.

54

If the Chief had been a great figure, Loomis filled the minds of people a lot more. Whatever the Chief had been, Loomis had finally put him down. And, now that I saw him, I believed everything that I had heard about his wonderful cleverness, his courage, his fighting qualities. There was not even a scar on him, men said, and that was why a good many believed in the superstition that he had found a way of avoiding bullets.

Well, there I stood in front of that gray cat of a man who, if he had known my real name, would have filled me full of lead. As it was, I answered him in the only way I could.

"This sort of knocks the wind out of me, Loomis," I said. "But I'd like to work for you, if you want me."

"What's your name?" he asked me.

"Richard Willis," said I.

"What have you done?"

"Punched cows."

"And men?"

"Well—" said I, and shrugged my shoulders.

"I don't want you," said Loomis, "until I've found out what you're good for. Understand?"

"I understand," said I.

Here Sue Carr put in, to say: "You'd better not join him till you've found what *he's* good for, Dick Willis."

He turned his head so gradually that, when he faced her, he still seemed to have an eye on me.

"You like eagle shooters, Sue, don't you?" said he.

She stared back at him, then glanced towards me. I could tell, with amazement, that she was not the least afraid of him.

"I like Dick Willis," she answered. "I don't want to see him throw in with you, Harry."

"We don't know that he'll be asked to throw in with me," replied Loomis. "We'll have to find a little job for him, as a test."

Carr sat up suddenly.

"It's cold as the devil!" he declared, with a shudder in his voice.

He stood up. As a matter of fact, there was not a breath of wind stirring, and the hollow hand of the valley retained all the heat of the sun, though the sun itself was now well down below the real horizon, and only the red fire of it kept burning up behind the mountains, making them stand near and black. It was a time of the day when a man could have lain down on the ground without a coat on his back and watched the stars come out, the way children do. But Carr declared that he was cold, and invited all of us to come into the house.

Now that he was standing, I could see what a real colossus he was. He must have been six or seven or even eight inches over six feet, but I could not be sure, because he had emphasized his altitude by wearing boots with exceptionally high heels. He made Loomis seem like a little boy.

"I can't go in," said Loomis.

"I'm going to make a bowl of punch," answered Carr. "You better stay."

"No," answered Loomis. "I'm on the way to Blue Water."

Carr whistled. "That's bad business for you," he suggested.

"Nobody else can do it," said Loomis. "Little Charlie is on a rampage. He's raising the devil, I hear, and I'll have to collect him and take him back with me. It's his regular annual tear."

"You've got to stay and drink some punch with me," replied Carr.

"I can't," said Loomis. He looked at the girl, not at her father. Even after he had risen, she remained bowed over his empty chair, as though she were brooding deeply.

Now she raised her head, but her eyes said nothing to Loomis.

"You can stay, all right," said Carr, chuckling. He pointed his immense beam of an arm at me and said: "Send Willis down there to get Little Charlie. You want to test the lad. Why not send him along?"

56

"Send him to get Charlie?" said Loomis, with a twisted smile.

"Why not?" asked Carr.

"Well, why not," answered Loomis. I saw a cruel flash in his face, and knew that I was in for it. Then he added: "You might as well go down to Blue Water and get Little Charlie for me, Willis. That would be enough of a test of you, I suppose."

The cold chills began to work in me. But what could I do? From every viewpoint, things were going well, according to the theory on which I'd ridden into the mountains with Ferrald. My first impulse had simply been to get him away from my brother, but now that we were in the mountains it was pretty impossible to shake Ferrald off. Even at this moment he was probably lurking somewhere near by, waiting for a chance to speak to me, and if I told him that I actually had a chance to join the gang, he would be in a seventh heaven of happiness, of course. If the two of us were to find a chance to revenge the death of Jerry Ferrald, there was no better way than that of working from the inside.

I had to answer: "I'll go bring Little Charlie. How'll I know him?"

"He asks how he'll know Little Charlie," said Loomis, turning to Carr with his cruel, faint smile.

Carr thundered out a laugh. "You'll know him by his roaring," said he. "And then, when you see him, you'll be spotting a man about my size, but not much older than you are. You'll know Little Charlie. He ought to just about fit into your mind!"

CHAPTER X

THE TRAIL TO BLUE WATER

CARR and Loomis went on toward the house, the vast hand of Carr resting on the shoulder of Loomis. I stood there looking down at my toes, measuring myself, and seeing that I was up against a hopeless proposition. When I looked up, the girl was right in front of me. There was a sort of pity in her eyes, but there was a savage gleam, too. She was a wild Indian, all right.

"Well?" she said. "You know the trail to Blue Water?"

"No," said I.

"Keep straight down the canyon beyond the lake," she told me. "Never leave the main gulch, and you'll come out at Blue Water. It's not far away."

"All right," said I.

I started to turn toward the corral where my horse was grazing. Susan Carr came along with me, and I went slowly enough, you can be sure.

"Is he really as big as your father?" I asked.

"Within ten pounds," she answered, "and every bit of him is hard."

I felt the keen, Indian look in her eyes again.

"All right," I muttered.

She leaned against the corral fence and watched me daub a rope on my mustang and saddle up. When I had climbed aboard the horse, she came up and held out her hand.

"Good luck," said she.

"Thanks, Sue," said I. "Luck is what I'll need, I guess, if I'm going to make it."

She kept hold of my hand, and now she gave it a little shake, as though to rouse me.

"You know something?" she asked. "He's a bull!"

"That sure cheers me up a lot," said I.

"It ought to. There are always ways of handling bulls. They close their eyes when they charge."

"What?"

"If you wave a red flag at 'em long enough, in just the right way, they charge, and close their eyes."

I stared down at her. She was shining with her idea, and I saw the point of it well enough. If a man can be badgered to a certain point, he makes a fool and a bad fighter of himself. But still, when I considered wading in

58

on a man the size of Carr and the character of a Loomis outlaw, I couldn't see myself winning out.

"I'll try to play my hand, one way or another," said I.

"Are you very much afraid?" she asked.

"I'm so scared that I'm sick at the stomach," said I.

She let my hand go, and stepped back from me.

"That's a pity," said Susan Carr coldly. "So long—and good luck," she said, without the slightest feeling, and I started on my way knowing that she already had begun to despise me.

It was depressing, all right. I began to see that the one thing for me to do was simply to ride straight out of the Blue Waters and go back home. I was still thinking of that, as I drifted the mustang down the gulch toward Blue Water, with the twilight thick and soft in the valley around me, and some of the upper mountain peaks still half rosy and shining with the last of the sunset glow.

And then a voice cracked in my ears, saying: "Hands up! And make it snappy!"

I swiveled around in the saddle with my Colt in my hand, my body bent over, instinctively ready to shoot. But I could see nothing but huge boulders along the wall of the gorge.

"All right, kid," said the voice—which I recognized now—and from behind one of those big rocks rode Ferrald. He was laughing and nodding his head in the gloom. "That was a fast draw. You've got the old fighting blood in you, son!"

I could have told him that I had been so much buried in my other fears that I had hardly had time to be alarmed by this flurry. However, I kept my mouth shut, while he ranged up beside me and asked:

"What's the news that you gathered out of the girl? You were long enough with her."

"I picked up a few things," said I, holding out on him. A funny thing that I wanted to impress that murdering crook of a Ferrald, but I did, after all!

"Yeah, you ought to 'a' got a chance to put up in the

house to-night," said Ferrald. "Then you could have picked up a handout and smuggled it to me, maybe!"

"Maybe," said I.

"Well," said Ferrald, "a kid like you may be as game as they make 'em, but he ain't likely to know how to handle jobs like this. Takes experience to make a gent into a good spy. But tell me what you found out, and where you're bound."

"I'm bound for Blue Water," said I.

"Why? Why Blue Water?"

"To get a man."

"What man?"

"Name of Little Charlie."

"Him? That big ox of a man? Loomis himself would have a job collecting Little Charlie!"

"That's what he said."

"Who said?"

"Loomis," I answered as calmly as I could.

"Loomis? What the devil are you talking about? Loomis said what? When?"

"Just now. He said that he's the only one that could handle Little Charlie. But he would let me try my luck."

Ferrald grabbed the reins of the horse and stopped me.

"You mean to say that you've been talking with Harry Loomis?" he demanded huskily.

"Yes."

"With Loomis!" breathed Ferrald. "What did he—why didn't you tell me right away? What's this business about going for Little Charlie?"

"It's my test. If I bring Little Charlie safely back to that place, I can join up with the gang of Loomis. That's my ticket."

Suddenly Ferrald threw his long arms into the air, shutting and opening his hands as though he were crushing throats.

"Then we've got 'em!" he shouted.

"It means that we've got a chance, anyway," said I.

"Kid, you're a wonder! But, great Scott, how can you

manage Little Charlie? He'd smash you—and me, too!"

"I might bluff him with a gun."

"Bluff him? He'd make you eat that gun—and digest it, too! We'll have to work together on him."

"That's no good," I thought out loud. "It has to be a one-man job, or it's not worth a rap."

"That's true," agreed Ferrald. "Got any plans?"

"No real ones. But you'd better go back and watch the house, yonder. It belongs to a big whale called Ralph Carr. Go on and keep an eye on that place, because Carr is in there drinking punch with Loomis."

Jim Ferrald began to curse through his clenched teeth. He said that he perhaps could go back and shoot Loomis from the dark.

"But what's the good in that?" said Ferrald finally. "I want 'em to taste the death that's coming their way, and to know *why* it's coming! But look here, kid. Why ain't the Chief showed up in Culver Canyon? You left the right word for him, didn't you?"

"Sure I did," I lied. "Have you been waiting down there?"

"I been down there," said Ferrald. "After I spotted you to the house by the lake, alongside of the girl, I went down into the canyon, and there wasn't a sign of anything, and then, as I was comin' back, I heard your hoss clickin' his hoofs against the rocks, and I ducked out of sight, was all. But it's funny that the Chief don't turn up!"

He growled out the last words.

I said: "It *is* funny that he don't come. Why do *you* think?"

Ferrald considered for a minute.

"*One* thing I know," he told himself, as well as me. "He's not staying because he's afraid. Because trouble is what he loves, and after staying away from it for three years, he must be dead crazy for a fight! Likely he's shaping up his plans and gathering some gents together, and when he strikes, he'll scoop the whole Loomis outfit right off the face of the earth. Don't you worry about him!"

"All right," said I, "only it looks sort of queer to me."

"What d'you expect?" said Ferrald. "Don't start trying to see through the brain of your brother, because you'll never get to the other side of him. He's deep, the Chief is. Leave *me* to do the worrying about whether he comes or not."

I was glad enough to let Ferrald argue in favor of the Chief; it took that burden off my own shoulders. Jim agreed that he couldn't help me with this particular job in Blue Water. He pointed out that I was a fool even to try such a thing, and he swore that he'd seen the hand of Little Charlie break a horseshoe. However, I could do my best, and if Loomis knew the sort of a beating I took before I was knocked senseless, perhaps he would let me get to the inside of the gang.

"The only thing is," said Ferrald, "that he might kind of forget himself, and tear *you* in two in the middle of warming up. So long. I'm going back to hang around that house."

He disappeared up the ravine, and I waited for a minute, unable to nerve myself to go one way or the other. Finally my mustang took the decision out of my hands by heading down the canyon toward Blue Water. It was a queer feeling, as though Fate had started thumping that horse like a burro on a mountain trail, with me for the senseless pack in the saddle, sealed up to be delivered in Blue Water for a mauling at the hands of Little Charlie.

I kept thinking about him all the way to the lights of the town, and the more I thought, the more clearly I saw the bulk and the loom of him in my imagination.

Well, I took the trail around the edge of the lake that gave the town its name, and saw the little, thin rays of yellow lights tremble and skip across the tops of the waves. And when I got into the edge of Blue Water, I heard Little Charlie, all right.

It was like the sound the wind makes when it booms far away, as if it were underground or behind a mountain, and all at once it jumps into the tops of the trees right over your head, crashing and roaring. That was the way that I heard Little Charlie. And the door of a saloon split open, and a jam of half a dozen men exploded out of it, some running right, and some running left, and some bolting across the street. Out behind the fleeing men leaped the giant, and caught the last pair, and knocked their heads together, and dropped them into the dust.

He stood a moment, afterwards, turning from side to side, as though wondering whether it were worth while to go after the others. It seemed to me that he was looking right at me, and seeing me clearly as my fool of a mustang carried me straight on, step after step, into Blue Water.

Finally Little Charlie turned around like a bear that has come out of its den to blink at the outer light, and went into the saloon, and the two men he had dropped remained motionless in the street. I wondered if he'd cracked their skulls!

CHAPTER XI

THE BULLY

THEY were alive. They got up, one after the other, just as I reached the spot, and went off holding their heads with their hands. One of them said that he had a fractured skull, that he could hear the edges of the bone grating together, and that he was going to die, sure. The other one said that he was going to get a gang together and come back and kill Little Charlie. But it didn't interest me a great deal to hear them. If I had thought that the gang might arrive, I would have waited and let anything that was in the cards happen to Little Charlie, with the hope that I might then be able to take the remnants or the hulk of him back to the house of Ralph Carr. But I knew, in the bottom of my boots, that this was just talk that I'd been hearing, and that nothing whatever would come of it.

Well, I tied that mustang to the hitch rack, and I tied it as a horse was hardly ever tied before. Because I told myself that after that knot was tied I would have to walk straight into the saloon and start my work. So I tied, and retied the lead rope, until finally I had used up the tail of it, and had to face the light that split through and spilled over the swinging doors.

It was only ten steps to those doors, but it took me five minutes to get there, because I had to slow up to settle my hat on my head, and to pull up my belt a couple of notches, and to set my bandanna straight, and to dust off my sleeves. But finally I had to get through those doors.

They shut behind me and made a *swish-swish* that seemed to hiss in my ears. "Silly fool! Silly fool!" they seemed to say.

Oh, I was a silly fool, all right, because now I could see Little Charlie as well as hear him. He had a voice good enough for a pair of fighting bulls, when they heave and thunder and groan at each other in the spring of the year, and sweat and bump and shake the ground with their roaring. But the voice of Little Charlie was nothing compared with the look of him.

Yes, he was as big as Ralph Carr, but the size of him was not muffled or obscured or overlaid with any fat, and his hide fitted over his muscles like thin, pink rubber on the stretch. His clothes couldn't disguise what he was. His shoulders looked right through the cloth; the bulge of his neck had burst his collar wide open. The heads of the other men moved small and foolish about the level of his shoulders, or lower than that, so that I could get a fair look at his face. And what a face!

Like Samson, he must have put his trust in the length of his hair. In knots and strings and pale, blond masses it fell down over his neck. No hat could sit very long on the bulk of that hair without being bounced off. And across his upper lip there stretched a couple of pale ropes of mustache. His mouth was big enough to bite off the leg of a horse. It was red, and always bright with liquor and the steam of his own engine, and the fire that burned in him kept flashing in his eyes.

That was the man I was to take back to the house of Ralph Carr!

Well, I smiled a little to myself, a sick smile, and went up to the bar to get a drink. I needed one!

It was a queer thing to see a score or so of men hanging around that big, dangerous devil. Half a dozen of them had been kicked out of the place a few minutes before, but the rest of these muckers kept hanging around to admire the giant, and enjoy the pleasure of electric vibrations that kept them shaking in their boots. They were drinking his liquor, but it wasn't the pleasure of the whisky that kept them there. As fast as the liquor blew them hot, Little Charlie blew them cold.

I had a bare chance to get to the bar and have a squint at my pug-nosed mug in the mirror, and wonder why the skin was brown, instead of yellow, green, and white, the way I felt. And I had a chance to recall what the girl had said to me—that the way to fight a bull was to wave a red flag at it till it went blind with anger.

She was right. But to wave a rag at this monster seemed like standing in front of a stampeding herd. That's what he seemed like. A crowd, not one man. A bull was what he was, though. His eyes were prominent, like the eyes of a bull. They were very wide apart. The only small thing about him was his forehead, and the eyes were set in the corners of it, so that it seemed that he could look backward as well as forward.

I say that I just had time to get set at the bar, but when I asked for a drink, the bartender gave me a sick grin and shook his head.

"Everything's on Little Charlie," he said.

Well, that was my chance to start bluffing, and I took a deep breath and started in. I brought out my voice with a loud bawling note in it, though I was crumbling to bits under the breastbone.

"On Charlie?" I said. "I don't drink with gutter-pups!"

The bartender sagged. His knees had buckled under him a little. I could feel the silence wash away from me in a wave until it reached Little Charlie.

"Who ain't drinking with me?" he bellowed. "Show me the poor half-wit of a maverick that don't know that this is my water hole, because I'm goin' to put my brand on him!"

He started for me, as he said this, and the other men between us scattered away as though he were a wind, and they were paper images.

It was a bad minute, but I barked out, without turning my head—I could see the whole picture in the mirror— "Put on the brakes, you lumbering load of junk. If you bump into me, I'll tear you apart!"

Those words actually stopped him short. Then he let out a whoop that still makes the nerves of my ears tremble when I think of it, and he started for me again, with one hand made into a fist as big as my head.

I pulled the revolver out from under my armpit and laid it on the bar, and the flash of the Colt brought a deep, gasping cry from those welshers who were in the barroom with me. The flash of it stopped Little Charlie again, too. He reached for his own gun, but I was saying to the scared bartender:

"Here, you! Take this gun of mine again, and put it away from me. Because I might be tempted to use the butt of it on this bull calf. And I don't want to finish him that fast. I want to see how long he'll last against my fists! I want to use my hands on him. Now trot out that drink of whisky!"

The bartender took the gun with both hands, as though it were red-hot, and put it away beneath the bar.

Little Charlie shouted: "Turn around and lemme at you, or I'll knock your head off from behind!"

"You dirty crook," I said, "the only way you ever won a fight was by hitting a man from behind. You wouldn't dare to look a man in the eye, and then lift a fist. Bartender, give me that drink!"

"I wouldn't dare? Listen!" boomed Little Charlie, turning to the others. "He says I never tackled a gent from in front. He don't know that I just now heaved six bums out of this dump! He don't know—"

I had the whisky bottle, now, and I filled myself a good drink with it, and curled my left hand around the neck of the bottle.

"They don't have any real men in Blue Water," I cut in on Little Charlie. "When I get through with this drink, I'm going to turn around and bust you wide open. And the yellow inside you is going to run all over the floor, and the stuffing is going to come out."

I heard strangling sounds. Then in the mirror I saw the terrible image of Little Charlie dancing up and down and throwing out his arms and yelling:

"Turn around now! Turn around now! I'm goin' to twist your head off your neck. I'm goin' to kill you like a woman wrings the head off a chicken. I swear I'm goin' to tear your head off you the same way!"

He was panting and blowing. I sipped my drink without any hurry and said to his image in the glass:

"When I turn around, you'll wish that you'd never dared to leave the barn you belong in and pretend to be a man. Bartender, here's to you. I hope I don't dirty your floor with the grease of that big hulk, but if I do, I'll mop it up with his carcass."

The bartender looked at me and then he looked at the immensity of Charlie, and finally, out of the throat of the bartender there came a crazy, squeaking, tearing laughter.

Little Charlie reeled back, as though he'd been struck with a club. It was plain hysteria that made that bartender laugh, I know, but Charlie thought that he was the point of the joke, and it fairly took the wind out of him.

He swung around and looked to see whether or not any of the others were laughing. He turned so suddenly that his hair swung out behind his head, something like the skirts of a woman when she pirouettes. And the rest of the men in that barroom, they began to laugh, too.

It fairly dazed me. The picture in the mirror blurred, for a minute, I was so astonished. But I suppose they'd been loathing that bully all the time, and now they were beginning to *hope,* at least, that he might get what was coming to him, and that they could indulge in a little laughter at his expense. Anyway, there they were, every one of them laughing his head off. And Little Charlie glared around him with the confused and bulging eyes of a madman.

"You wanta laugh?" he gasped out—and his gasp was like the panting of a steam engine, with the thrust of a piston against the pressure. "You wanta laugh? I'll give you a chance to laugh. When I get through breakin' him up, I'm goin' to break up some of the rest of you. I'm goin' to tear the hearts out of you, you dirty lot of—"

"Shut up, Charlie," said I. "You'll need all your wind before I'm through with you!"

"Save your breath, Charlie," said one of the men. "Maybe he's a champion prize fighter. He looks like it."

"Maybe he's a jujutsu expert," said another.

"Whadda I care about the prize fighters and the jujutsu fakers?" roared Little Charlie, beginning to sway from side to side. "I'll take on a crowd of 'em. I'll bash their heads in for 'em. I'm goin' to squeeze the juice out of this here, and see what's the color of it! I'm goin' to—"

"There you go," said I, suddenly turning around to face him. "But talking won't win this fight."

When he saw me face him, he gave out a frightened screech and started for me, his feet slipping on the boards, he was in such a hurry. He was a terrible thing to see. The image of him in the mirror had been bad enough, but eye to eye with him, I saw that he was half crazy with fury, mad with being doubted, and his ropy mustache was wet with the steam of his panting.

As he charged, I just hunched my coat off my shoulders and started slowly to pull my arms out of the sleeves, so that I stood there helpless in front of him. Little Charlie might knock me silly with a punch, of course, but in the West, fights are fought fair. And if the crowd thought that he was taking an advantage of me, he wouldn't have time to hit more than one blow before some one whanged him over the head with a chair.

68

As he charged, in fact, a chorus yelled at him:

"Leave him alone till he's got his hands free, Charlie!"

Perhaps Charlie would have stopped out of a sense of fair play, anyway, but I doubt it. Not from the way he was lurching in at me, with wild eyes rolling. But public opinion had enough force to clear up his brain for an instant and halt him. He was almost on top of me, before he stopped himself, teetering on his toes, his arms flung out over my head to keep his balance. Then he staggered back, and I slipped the coat off over my hands.

CHAPTER XII

THE FIGHT

THAT had to be the start, it seemed. There I was with my hands free, and facing him, and you'd think that I'd have to begin the fight, at last. But I saw another way to delay it and to whip him with words some more.

So I said, as I put my coat on the bar:

"Take your coat off, Charlie. And your guns, too. Or I might be tempted to take 'em away from you and shove 'em down your throat."

He swayed back and forth, and I thought that he was going to rush right in at me, but instead of that, he began to take my advice, and to laugh.

The whole crowd had started laughing, at this last crack of mine, and yet all of their laughter together was nothing compared with the maniacal outburst that flooded the throat of Charlie and went whooping and shrieking and booming through the roof of that place. The whole building trembled. The whole of *me* trembled, at least.

Charlie, taking my advice, whipped the pair of guns out of his holsters and threw them down on the floor. Then he grabbed his coat to take it off, but he simply ripped it in two with the terrible force of his hands. It made me sick to see—because that was as heavy cloth

69

as you would find. But it went like paper under his touch.

He tore that coat off in two halves. Then he held out his hands toward me, making them alternately into fists, and swaying back and forth and moaning with every breath he drew.

"Now!" he shouted. "Are you ready?"

"Ready to knock your head off!" said I, and I stepped one pace out from the bar toward him.

He made a gigantic bound to reach me with a punch that looked like a moving house as it came through the air. There was no trouble getting away from it, and as the mass of him went by, I aimed for my target, his right eye, and let him have everything that was in me. That was my only hope—to close both those eyes, and leave him floundering in the dark. That was his weak spot. He had no beetling brows to protect the eyes. And I began to have a little glimmering of hope as I felt the knuckles of my fists bite through the shallow flesh against the bone.

Little Charlie went by me like an express train, crashed against the bar, and tilted the whole mass of it far over. A horde of bottles and glasses crashed to the floor inside, but on my honor that noise was nothing compared to the uproar the men of Blue Water made when they saw Charlie turn again, with one eye blurred over and dripping red down his cheek.

Charlie made not a sound that I could hear. If he had looked like a maniac before, he looked like a fiend out of hell, now. He pointed me out with his left hand and ran at me with his right. I feinted to dodge to my left again. He was so blind with his fury that he half turned and let his punch go so that it missed my head more than a foot, and I let him have a beauty over the left eye as he hurtled past me.

He skidded into the table in the corner and crashed it into kindling wood, and went down in the heap of the ruins. The men of Blue Water were dancing, screeching idiots, by this time.

"It's a clean knock-down!" the fools yelled.

I looked down at my right hand and saw that the blood from my sliced and bruised knuckles was running down over the tips of my fingers. Yet I felt no pain from that hand. Only I knew that if I used it once or twice more against the stone wall of that forehead, I would smash in the knuckles.

Little Charlie got up with the wreckage dripping off him and both his eyes a bloody mess. He tried to wipe the blood out of them but only got the salt of his sweating hands into the wounds, I suppose. Because he leaped straight up into the air, and as he landed, he was running for me the third time, still silent, though his face was stretched and his mouth frozen open as though on a frightful screech.

I could tell by the way he aimed at me that he was half-blinded now. But in spite of that, he was more dangerous, because he was coming in not with his fists, but with his open hands, and I knew that if he got so much as a finger tip on any solid part of me, he'd soon have me down, crunching my bones.

It wasn't so hard to dodge him, though, and as I dodged, I hammered at his left eye again, and got it with the full swing of my left, so hard that my arm went numb to the elbow. At the same time one of his grabbing hands caught me by the shoulder. If his finger tips had been hooked in, that would have been the end of me, but as it was, I slipped from under, and he only got the bark in his hands.

What I mean to say is that the grip of that hand ripped the shirt and the undershirt right off my back, and the back pull of his arm slung me skidding across the floor and against the wall.

I'm not a lightweight, even if I'm not so tall, but he threw me across that room as though I had been a lap dog.

I got up to my feet in a scramble, scared to death, ready to yell for help. I saw the men of Blue Water standing agape. The monster was rushing at me for the fourth time.

71

That was when I had a touch of a clever idea. That ravening beast that came for me could not see a thing out of his puffing left eye, by this time, and out of his right eye he probably was seeing only a blur. Of course his judgment of distance was ruined. So instead of getting away from the wall, I took the chance of being pinned against it, and stood right there, as though I were dazed. I had my knees bent under me ready to spring to either side, but I suppose that it looked as though I were ready to drop in a collapse, because I heard the men of Blue Water yelling at me to get away from the wall. But I stood right there, and saw the distorted face of Charlie writhe into a look of joy as he lurched in at me.

At the last minute, I jumped to the side. His hand brushed right against my face—it was like being grazed by a beam—and he crashed full face into that wall.

I was away, and dancing on my toes, as I saw him turn again, so dazed that his hands were only half-raised. It was a brutal thing to do, but just then I was dealing with a brute. So I took a step forward and hammered my bruised right hand against the battleship prow that was his chin.

His head jammed back against the wall with a force that knocked down a small shower of plaster. It was as though he had been hit with two clubs, at once, a lighter one on the jaw and a heavier one on the base of the brain. Even then he did not crumple at once. He simply leaned forward, and put out his hands.

I was in a frenzy. It was now or never, to finish him. I gathered every scrap of my strength and slashed him across the jaw with both fists, right on the button.

Still he stood there, only with his mouth hanging open, his jaw pitched crookedly to the side as though it had been broken, while he looked at me out of those horrible things that were not like eyes at all, but a child's patched up water color of what eyes might be.

If he didn't go down this time, he wouldn't go down at all, I felt. But while I watched him, with helplessness coming over me, at last I saw his great knees bend. Perhaps he was crouching to hurl himself at me?

No, for his hands were sinking, too. In my ears the yelling of the men of Blue Water was a frenzy, as that mighty body suddenly crumpled up and pitched forward and struck the floor with an impact that knocked the dust up in long thin clouds out of the cracks between the boards.

He just lay there on his face, and suddenly I could feel not the hands of the men of Blue Water, as they patted my naked back, but the pain of my battered hands, and the sting where his terrible grip had taken a lot of hide off my shoulder.

I borrowed some cord and was about to tie the hands of Charlie behind his back, but I thought better of it. If there were to be anything more than a trick to the beating of him, I would have to take him back with me as though I could *never* be afraid of him. After all, I knew that it *was* only by using tricks that I had beaten him, and that a girl had told me how to win.

So I just stuffed the cord into my pocket and asked some of the men to turn him over on his back.

They did that, while I got on the torn rags of my shirt and then put on my coat. I took my gun. I picked up his two Colts and laid them on the bar.

A lot of the gang were offering me drinks, but I took just one before Charlie came to.

He sat up, bracing himself on his huge, trembling arms, and just sat there and blinked his swollen eyes, and shook his head because everything was darkness in front of him. I got a wet towel and tied it around his head. He groaned with the comfort of that coldness.

I left the towel on. It blinded him, but he was almost blinded, anyway, by what he'd suffered from my knuckles. I heaved at one of his thick arms, and he pulled up on his feet, and stood there, swaying, never saying a word. There was a good deal of blood on his mustache and some on his hair. I got another wet towel and wiped him as clean as I could, and then put his coat on over his arms, and tied it together down the back. Then I pushed his two revolvers into the holsters on his thighs. The barrels of those guns were three inches longer than common. They were made-to-order tools to fit his hand with butts that I couldn't have got my fingers around. Even the trigger guard was extra size.

One of the men started to make a speech and said that there was only one place for a ruffian like Little Charlie, and that was dangling at the end of a rope. And if one rope wouldn't hold his weight, they'd braid two together, and let him hang somewhere so that people could see him in the morning, and learn from the sight that it doesn't pay to be a bully, no matter what your size happens to be.

The men of Blue Water took up with that idea, in a hurry. They wanted to hang Little Charlie then and there. But I felt that I had bluffed so much that I could bluff a little bit more.

"You fellows back up," I said. "Charlie's had enough for one night. And now he's going home—with me. Unless some of you want to argue the point a little!"

No, they didn't want to argue the point. They'd been too excited, all of them, to realize that I'd beaten poor Charlie simply by skipping around and letting his own weight kill him. Just then, I suppose that I looked pretty big to them, though I was so shaky that I had to talk low for fear that even my voice would start trembling.

Well, I got Charlie out into the street. Somebody pointed out his horse to me, and he climbed into the saddle. I took the reins of his horse, then I got onto my mustang—and that was the way that we rode out of Blue Water into the night. By the starlight I looked at the huge bulk of that silhouette which drifted along beside me, and I saw the white of the towel that was still tied across his battered eyes.

I began to feel dizzy. I began to see what a gulf I'd walked across, and that only the steadying hand of that girl, Sue Carr, had ever brought me to the safe side of the tight rope.

CHAPTER XIII

THE RETURN

ALL the way to the Carr house, Little Charlie talked hardly at all. We were halfway there before he said: "Seems like I got my guns on me, again."

"You've got them," said I.

Then, a little later, we rode through a shallow runlet of water, and when he heard the splash of it, he said that he wanted to get off. I halted the horses while he got down, soaked the towel, and washed his eyes again and again, grunting and groaning a little as the cold of the water touched his wounded flesh.

Afterwards, he said that he could see a little, so I gave him the reins of his horse, and I rode ahead, when the trail narrowed here and there. He might, of course, pull out a gun and shoot me through the back. But I had a feeling that he would do nothing like that, and that the brain inside his great skull was too busily occupied with pondering on the strange events that had happened to him for him to try his hand at any more action.

"You been in the ring?" he said, after a time.

"No," said I, and I heard him clucking his tongue against his palate, like a thoroughly puzzled man.

We were in sight of the lighted windows of the Carr house before he spoke again.

"Don't seem like you got the shoulders to have such a punch," said Little Charlie.

If I had been honest, I would have told him that I had done very little except to peck away at his poor eyes, and that the solid wall was the chief thing that had knocked him out. But I couldn't afford to be honest—not by a long shot. Just now, I had to use everything that was possible in order to pull through this scrape.

When we got up close to the house, I said:

"Charlie, you're all sort of messed up. You'd better not

75

go in and let those people see you. The girl will be there, and your chief is there, and so is Carr, of course. You don't want all of those people seeing you like this, do you?"

"No," said he. "That wouldn't be much of a party for me. But how did all of this come about, eh?"

"Why," said I, "it was this way—Loomis heard that you were having a big bust in Blue Water and that you wouldn't come home. So he sent me down to bring you back."

"He sent *you?* Then he knew that you'd be able to bring me?"

"He sent me, anyway," said I.

"Then it's all right," said Little Charlie. "If he knew that you could bring me, he knew the sort of a gent that you are. I'm kind of wondering what would happen if you and Loomis was to tangle together. I ain't so sure that he'd come out on top!"

I grinned a little, at this, but the grin was all on one side of my face, you can be sure!

But the main point was that Charlie insisted on coming right in with me.

We turned the horses loose, and carried the saddles and bridles around through the kitchen door, and hung them up in the open hallway that hitched the kitchen to the rest of the house. Then we went back into the kitchen and washed our faces.

The big Negress, Aunt Lizzie, gave us both a look. She was as calm as you please, but she squinted pretty hard at the bleeding knuckles of my hands and the swollen, purple eyes of poor Charlie. She got some caustic and some other stuff that seemed to burn my fingers off, and on top, she laid down thin strips of sticking plaster. And she doctored the eyes of Charlie, too, till he teetered up and down on his toes with the stinging pain of her doctoring.

She just kept muttering with her thick lips: "That'll teach you to go around fightin', you rapscallion, you.

76

That'll teach you! What you been doin'? What hoss has been kickin' you in the face?"

"Him," said Little Charlie. "This here!"

He pointed at me, and Aunt Lizzie opened her eyes wider and wider, until they were all whites and no pupils, like the eyes of a statue.

"That little feller?" said she.

"He looks small only when he's standin' still," said Little Charlie. "When he starts movin', he starts expandin', and growin', and he keeps on growin' until he's as big as a house!"

It was strange to see the way he took the thing—as though it were a matter of course, and as though he felt little or no shame over it. He had been beaten, but he had been beaten by a man who was so well-known to be formidable, that his chief had sent down the new champion for that express reason.

It was miraculous to Little Charlie that any one could handle him, in this fashion. But what he wondered at was simply the miracle; he didn't pause a moment on the shame of his defeat.

After we were patched up a little, Aunt Lizzie told us to scoot into the dining room and eat, because she said that the venison steaks were pretty nearly all eaten, and getting cold.

And we went in.

I'll never forget the picture.

Ralph Carr filled almost the width of the long table, at one end, with his three hundred pounds and his beard, and his enormous, moving arms. At the other end of the table no one was placed, but the girl and Loomis were both up near the head. And when we came in, every man jack of 'em all jumped up to their feet.

The girl was the first, with a sharp little cry, and a few running steps to meet us, before she paused with one hand out before her. After her, big Carr pushed himself up on his legs. And last of all, even Loomis rose, and looked at Little Charlie out of his narrowed eyes, before he looked at me.

"Hullo, Harry," said Charlie. "The gent you sent got me, all right. He's gotta say that I kept on fightin' till I couldn't fight no more. He had to knock me colder'n a rock before I seen that there was no use standin' up to him!"

Well, the three of them had nerves as steady as those of most people, I suppose, but I must say that they gaped at this. Then the girl began to smile a little, all with her eyes, and all straight at me.

Why, I forgot the sting of the raw places on my shoulder, and I forgot the ache of my bruised hands, and the burn of the caustic that Aunt Lizzie had daubed on. All that I could see was those eyes, and all that I could feel in the world was a sudden appetite for happiness, and a sense that I was going to have heaped platters of it before very long.

It was not like the way that Allardyce had shone her eyes at the Chief, mind you, but it was a steady sparkling, as though something had tickled Sue Carr a lot, and as though she were going to be able to enjoy it for a long time.

Then big Ralph Carr began to laugh. The long, rolling thunder of that laughter went booming through the room, like organ music.

"Sit down, boys," he said. "Sit down, the pair of you. You'll be hungry. Look at the hands of poor Willis, everybody! Do you mean to say that he didn't use a club on you, Charlie? You mean to say that he just laid you out with his hands?"

It seemed to me not a very tactful question to ask of a man who had been beaten. And when I thought of the shifts and dodges that I had used back there in the saloon to save my neck, I was thoroughly ashamed. But Little Charlie was not in the least embarrassed. "There's a lot of strange things," he declared. "Grizzly bears is stronger than me, even. But I've seen 'em caught and choked with one rope. I've seen that, on a good, sizable bear, too. But the rope was used by a gent that knew his business. And the fists that was used on me to-night was hung on the arms of a gent that knew his business, too."

"Oh, look!" shouted Carr. "The coat's been torn off his back!"

"I disremember the details of things," said Little Charlie.

That was how the story went the rounds that I had not only beaten Charlie senseless, but that I'd simply torn the coat off his back! I tried to deny that I'd done any such thing, but that was put down to modesty—or, more than modesty, to the possibility that I was ashamed that I had fallen into such a blind, fighting frenzy that I had even torn up a man's coat!

Well, it was a very queer thing for me to sit down at that table, I can tell you, and look at the girl, close beside me, seeing the slender brown of her hands and the way the flesh over the knuckles dimpled, now and then, and looking across at the narrowed eyes of Loomis, the man I had promised to kill, if I could manage it. And from there I looked down to the huge, bruised face of Little Charlie.

He was very busy with his food, working on it contentedly. He got hold of a batch of roast venison ribs and I could hear his teeth snip through the gristle, and then a slow crushing sound as his molars smashed the rib bones, and he sucked the marrow. He never lifted his eyes from his plate, while he was feeding. But none of these people looked at him with the slightest token of disgust. They seemed rather inclined to smile at him. And in spite of myself, I began to have a liking for him, too.

We finished dinner rapidly, as hungry men always do, and Little Charlie went off to bed. Five minutes later his snoring kept a deep, heavy vibration through the house, a thing to feel rather than to hear. Then Ralph Carr, although the evening was hardly chilly, wanted a fire. His daughter built a big, shining blaze on the open hearth at the end of the room and pulled up one of the canvas chairs for him. There he lolled back, with his legs and his hands stretched out to the blaze, and his eyes closed.

We were all very quiet. I sat in one corner, looking at the fire, and the girl sat in another corner, and Harry Loomis walked up and down the room smoking a cigarette, and making no noise as he stepped. I couldn't see why, because he was wearing ordinary boots and spurs, but the spurs didn't jingle, and the leather would not creak, and the high heels dropped on the floor as though onto thick felt. He raised not even a vibration of the boards, so far as I could see. A ghost could have walked like that, a gossamer thing. After a time, he said quietly: "We'll be riding early in the morning, Willis. Be ready. You're a regular man with me now."

So it was over, and I was an accepted member of the Loomis outfit! In fact, I was an accepted spy!

Loomis said a brief good night to Carr. In front of the girl he lingered for a moment. What he said puckered my skin, and slowed up the blood in my body. I can remember it as clearly as though it were five minutes ago. I can remember the silk of his voice, and the caress in it. I can remember thinking, suddenly, of the softness of a cat's paw, and the sharp nails under the velvet. But there was no call for any particular strangeness in his actions or in his voice, for his words were enough to drive nails through my heart.

"Are you going to kiss me good night, Sue?" he asked.

CHAPTER XIV

A NEW LIFE

No one was watching me, and yet I hardly dared to look across the room at the girl. She was sitting on a big, homemade chair, with her feet tucked up under her, in that way some women have. There was a big spread of elk horns high on the wall above her, and the mask of wild cat grinning and glaring close by, as she looked up at Loomis, for a moment. It was quite a long and silent moment, too. Then she uncurled herself and stood up, and lifted her face.

He leaned over her and kissed her, and went rapidly out of the room with his soundless step. The girl just stood there, with her hands clasped behind her, and her head still thrown back, and her eyes closed. And except for the crackling of the fire, anybody could have heard my heart bumping like the wheels over a log bridge.

Then Ralph Carr said: "Look here, Sue. Quit it."

My heart stopped bumping, and my blood went cold again. You see, he had his back turned to her, so how the devil could he make out what the girl was doing? But when he spoke to her, she tilted her head forward again and opened her eyes quite wide, and looked down at the floor.

"Are you getting tired of your man-killer, sneak-thief, and robber *par excellence?*" said Ralph Carr, in his thick voice, still spreading his immobile body in front of the fire.

She said nothing, but she looked at me.

"I'll go," I said, and stood up.

"You stay here, young man," commanded Carr. "Come over by the fire."

I went over by the fire, and stood with my hands behind me, trying to look composed, teetering back and forth from one foot to the other, and mighty nervous, you bet!

"You come over, too," said Carr. "Come along, honey."

"No," said the girl.

"Are you afraid of him?" asked Carr.

"Afraid of whom?" said she.

"Afraid of young Dick Willis?" said he.

"No, I'm not afraid," said the girl.

She came to the other side of his chair without looking at me, and faced her father. The firelight as it leaped made a rapid play of brightness and shadow over her body, so that she seemed to be breathing very quickly.

"You want to chuck Loomis and take this boy?" asked Carr, the thick lids of his eyes still closed.

"I want you to stop this," she directed firmly.

"He's not very pretty to look at," said Carr, "but he seems to be a man. How clean a man he is, I can't tell. But he seems to be a man. You want him, do you?"

"Yes, I want him," said the girl.

Just like that she said it, easily, smoothly, while something cracked at the base of my brain and sent sparks shooting through my mind.

"If you want him, you'll have him, I suppose," said Ralph Carr, yawning. "I'll tell Loomis that in the morning. After all, perhaps it's about time for me to do something."

He spread out the immensity of one hand and then gradually closed it.

I could see what he meant. He was quietly considering the possible necessity of fighting things out with Loomis. And I knew that that would be like a battle between a bear and a snake. The bear might have the strength, but he would lack the speed and the poison tooth. It was a queer thing that the argument seemed to be all between the girl and her father, and although I had been popped into a place of importance, nobody even looked at me.

"You can't handle Loomis," she said.

"Wait a minute. Did you *ever* care a rap about Loomis?" he asked.

"That's my business," said the girl.

He opened his eyes about halfway, and reached out and took her by the arm and pulled her close to him.

"The fact is that you've always been afraid of him, and detested him. Is that the straight of it?"

She was silent.

"You've pretended, just in order that life could be easier for me?"

Still she was silent.

"Well, then," said Carr, "I'll do something about Loomis!"

"You won't!" she insisted, with a sudden violence.

"Won't I?" said he, smiling.

His eyes opened big and full and bright, and I could see that for all his indolence, his sodden carelessness, his gross luxury of body, there was not a scruple of fear in him, and that he would lay down his life in the pinch for what he considered the best. He looked up at the girl, with his smile. She put her hand on the great breadth of that forehead of his, and smiled back down at him. All at once I knew that they were as close as grass and ground to one another.

"Wait," she cautioned him.

She came around his chair and stood in front of me and looked at me very thoughtfully.

"Well, Dick," she murmured, "what do you think? Do you want me?"

I muttered some unintelligible gibberish.

She turned back to her father and as she did so, she held out a hand rather absently toward me. I took hold of it.

"Yes," she said to Ralph Carr, "he seems to want me."

"Then I'll arrange things," said he, nodding at the fire.

I managed to find my tongue and say: "Perhaps I can do some of the arranging, Mr. Carr." My voice was absurdly small, and it shook.

The girl looked suddenly around, but there was no doubt or question in her eyes. She was simply smiling at me, and great doors opened, and all my soul went galloping out and stampeded into sunshine.

"We'll talk things over," said Sue. "Dick and I will talk things over."

Then I saw that I would have to speak, and tell them the truth about myself. But in an instant, I knew that I *couldn't* speak. All I could do was bite my teeth together, and groan, without making a sound. There was only one point that I could clear up for them, so I said:

"I want to make one thing straight. That's this. I didn't slam Charlie around, to-night. I did what Sue suggested to me. I simply got him so mad that he was half blind. And while he was half blind, I managed to make him all blind with a few punches. Then I had a lot of luck, and in the wind-up he went flat. It was all luck, and the advice that Sue gave me. Little Charlie—he could tear me in two, if he wanted to."

Now, as I got started on this speech, they both looked at me. But toward the end of it they both looked at one another, and began to smile a little, which made me feel foolish.

Then Carr stood up.

"We both know what to think of you, my lad," said he, stretching his bulk before the fire. "But now I'm going to bed. So long!"

He went out of the room, and I stayed behind, looking nervously at the girl.

Well, there was nothing sentimental about her attitude. She simply asked: "Will you tell me what brought you up here, Dick?"

"No," I answered. "I can't."

"Have you given us your right name?" she asked.

"One of them," said I.

"Well," said Sue Carr, "I'll be grateful for the half knowledge. And you won't be bothered if I don't chatter about father and me. Good night, Dick."

That was the way she left me, just pausing at the door to say over her shoulder:

"You'll find a lot of rooms with beds made up in them. Turn in wherever you please." And she was gone.

I didn't know much about such things, but I had always thought that when a man and a woman confessed they were fond of one another, there must be a certain solemnity about the time, and a certain silence, too, and a great deal of forward thinking. But up here in the Blue Water Mountains, everything seemed to be taken for granted.

I was so bewildered that I wanted to have more space around me. And that was why I walked out from the house into the open. It was only after I had a look at the moon that was walking up the sky between a pair of mountains, with the snowy summits like two triangular clouds beside it, that I remembered Ferrald, again, and my brother, and the whole of the queer tangle that had brought me to the house of Ralph Carr.

I felt that I had moved into a new house of life, and that there were bigger rooms in it than the old house to which I had been accustomed. I looked down on my past as if from the mountains onto a distant plain where the figure that had been my old self still seemed to be moving about in a small and futile way. My mother, too, seemed to be a thing remembered rather than real. Only the Chief, and his terrible need, was real and important as the people who were now around me.

Well, as I stepped out into the moonlight, with these feelings in my mind, something stirred to the left of me. It seemed some wild beast of the cat family climbing up the side of the house. But as I turned and looked, I saw that it was a man disappearing through a second-story window.

The sight of him put a gun into my hand, but on second thought I didn't shoot. I didn't even go back into the house to give an alarm. I don't know why I failed to do that. I simply felt that what happened in this house was already too strange for me to understand, and that I had better not puzzle my brain about it.

It's the clearest proof of what a strange outfit it was, that I allowed a thing like that to happen without rousing up the place. What I really felt, was that it was probably one of the stray men of Loomis, who had arrived late and would naturally expect the front door to be locked, so he had gone in by the second story.

I turned along the edge of the water, between the lake and the pine trees, and after a moment I heard a soft whistle. A shadow of a man stepped out from behind a tree.

"Jim?" I called, in a guarded voice.

"The same," said he.

He came up and stood close to me, with the attitude

of a man who is measuring himself against another. Then he shook his head.

"I seen what Little Charlie looked like, but I dunno how it happened," said he.

I shrugged my shoulders. "Never mind Little Charlie," said I. "The important thing is that the Chief hasn't shown up."

"Quit it, will you?" exclaimed Ferrald impatiently. "Mountains ain't made in a day, and plans like the kind that the Chief makes, they ain't framed in a second. Look at the Chief—what would it mean to him just to wipe out Loomis? No, sir. The Chief loved Jerry, between you and me, and he's goin' to smash the whole Loomis gang, now, to make up for the murdering of Jerry Ferrald. Just keep your hat on, and wait a while."

As long as Ferrald was willing to wait, of course I was happy enough to follow his good advice. Poor Ferrald could not know that I felt like an animal in a trap which would be sprung on me the moment it was found out that the Chief would *never* come up to this place of danger.

I told Ferrald the important stages of what had happened, and above all that Loomis had ordered me to be ready to ride in the early morning, and had said that I was a regular in his gang, now. Ferrald was delighted by this. He said that it made everything more and more perfect, and how delighted the Chief would be when he heard about it, because with me in the camp of the enemy, and with the Chief and Ferrald working on the outside, it would be a tremendous thing, an opportunity such as would not come twice in a lifetime, to gather the whole tribe together and then crush 'em!

I'll never forget how Ferrald closed his hands together and stamped a foot into the ground, as he said that. Jim was simply hungry for blood. He said that he would be ready to trail us, no matter where I rode with Loomis in the morning. And after he had spotted the hangout, which would probably be the central camp of the Loomis gang, he would then return to Culver Canyon and wait for the Chief and whatever men the Chief was bringing up with him.

I was pleased with this idea, and shook hands with Ferrald. He paid me a lot of compliments, and he could not get over the handling of Little Charlie. But he said that if he had thought twice, he would have remembered from the first that I was the brother of the Chief, and therefore that I was worth ten ordinary men.

When I got back into the house, I pushed open a door on the second story, and sure enough, by the moonlight that slid in through the window, I made out that it was a bedroom, and unoccupied. So I peeled, and turned into that bed, and as I went to sleep, I had a picture in my mind of a man galloping, galloping, galloping —always south and south, and that man was my brother, the Chief, getting farther and farther away from trouble, farther and farther away from that crazy man-killer of a Ferrald.

I decided, before sleep came over me, that if I could get through one more day, and keep Ferrald amused, I could be sure that the Chief would have had a sufficient head start, and that he would be safe from the man hunter.

CHAPTER XV

THE LOOMIS GANG

MOUNTAIN nights are nearly always cold. There was ice in the air when I got up the next morning. My hands were so sore that I could hardly pull on my boots, and my shoulder burned, and there seemed to be a drowsy fever in me. But I was dressed and out at the corral with my rope and saddle before the gray of the morning had more than started, while the stars were still shining and the mountains were just beginning to turn black against the east.

Loomis was already there. He made a gesture at me,

by way of good morning, then waved his rope at the bunch of horses he had cornered. They scattered into a fan, but his noose went out like a hand and snagged the one he wanted. He was saddled and mounted before I managed to catch my mean devil of a mustang. He had smoked most of a cigarette before Little Charlie appeared on a run, and rumbled an apology for being late as he jumped over the corral fence.

A moment later we were all on the trail.

It was a shifting, winding way under the pine trees, which kept the dark of the night huddled about their heads as though they hated the sun, and when we came out of the woods at last, at the first high divide, it was strange to see that the morning sky was all red and gold.

After that, we followed trails and no trails for about two hours, climbing most of the way, and rarely getting to a spot where a horse could gallop. In this way we came to a shallow little valley scooped out of a high plateau, with a bit of a lake spotted in the middle of it. The horse of Loomis whinnied so hard that it almost stopped walking, and by that I could guess that we had come to the central home of the Loomis gang.

We had talked very little on the way. I merely said to Loomis:

"How does big Ralph Carr figure? How does he fit in?"

"Carr wants nothing except a good chance to hunt and to fish, most of his days," Loomis said. "He sent his girl off to school and when she finished that, he felt that his duties in life were finished. He's either gone for a week at a time climbing above timber line and living on his rifle, or else he's lying about the house, taking the sun, or broiling himself in front of a fire. These Blue Waters are full of his cattle. You see those steers over yonder? They really belong to Carr. But he lets us eat them. He doesn't care. When he needs some hard cash, I help him out, and about the future he doesn't care a hang."

It was a queer picture to paint of a man, but I had

seen enough of Carr to guess that it was the truth.

As we went down the slope, I asked Loomis why he had picked out such an open place, with the cabin in plain sight, and with the trees mostly open groves of rather stunted timber. He said that it was true that a posse would be able to see his men from a distance, in a spot like that, but that his men would also be able to see the posse, if they had a fair break of luck. Besides he had his spies at work everywhere, and they were generally able to give warning before any important man hunt started in the direction of the Blue Waters.

I could see the point in this position, and it increased my respect for the brain of Loomis. The man himself I could not like, but his ideas were those of a fellow who is always willing to take the gambling chance.

Loomis gave me a final bit of advice, as we came down toward the camp.

"Willis," he said, "you have qualities, otherwise you wouldn't be here with me at this moment. Now, down there in the camp you'll find eight or ten fellows who are mostly as wild hawks. They'll be curious about you, because you're a new man. They'll probably test you in various ways. Don't lose your temper. Keep smiling, and keep your face shut most of the time. Otherwise, they're likely to tear you to pieces—and if there's a brawl inside my gang, I let the boys fight it out. When bad blood begins, it has to be spilled as quickly as possible. At least, that's my idea."

This was a rather grim introduction to the new life, but I set my teeth and swore that I would be able to go through with it. My limit was only one day, I told myself, and after that, I could fade out of this picture, and go on my own way.

Those fellows in the camp looked all right, when we rode up. The lookout had passed them the word, long before, and they came out of the big cabin into the brightness of the morning sun smoking their after-breakfast cigarettes. They waved their hands at us, and then a cluster gathered around Little Charlie. They failed to laugh at the sight of his swollen and discolored face, and when he told them with perfect frankness what had happened to him, they turned grave, bright eyes of inquiry on me.

I felt like a pigeon among so many hawks. The least of this group would be able to eat half a dozen fellows like me, either with a gun or with a knife. Even if it came to straight fists, any one of them would probably more than handle me. Out here in the open, I would not be able to play tricks on them.

So I seldom looked at their faces, because I knew that if I caught the eye of a man, the fear was apt to come up in mine. I kept my glances for whatever I was doing, went into the cabin, and put my pack in an empty bunk after I'd made sure that nobody claimed that place. Then I went out and hobbled my horse, which was the way they kept their saddle stock. And what mounts they had! Every one was hand-picked, and money had not been spared to fit the fancy. From mustang to thoroughbred, every horse that I laid an eye on shone with quality, until my sun-bleached runt of a broncho looked like an old rag in comparison.

I was put to work at once. Considering what those men were, it was plain that they could hardly hire a cook. The cooking was simply done in rotation by every member of the gang except Loomis. But the newest member was made into a roustabout to carry water, set the table, and peel potatoes and make himself useful in general. Being the newest member, of course, a lot of this work was passed over to me by the former roustabout.

He was a lad of only eighteen, extremely blond, with something weak about his mouth and something savage about his eyes. He gloried in seeing some one else take his place, and he stood about and laughed and gloated while I sat beside a potato sack and dropped peelings into one pan and the crystal-white of naked potatoes into the other. His name was Emory something or other. Most of the men simply called him Em for short.

The cook for the day was a sour-faced fellow two or three years older than me. He had been shot to pieces in gun fights and limped in both legs. In fact, he walked as though he had wooden legs from the knees down and were not sure where his feet would fall. There was a continual expression of pain and of derision in his face, as though he were sneering at his own sufferings, while he hobbled about the stove and got things ready for lunch. He had nothing to say to me except to give a few brisk orders. And I obeyed them without a word.

When lunch time came, I had to carry in the food. It was horribly cooked, but nobody complained, because the rule was that the first fellow who made a kick would have to do the cooking for three days, without relief. After lunch, we all went out and lay about half in the sun and half in the shadow of the pine trees. I went off by myself, smoked a cigarette, and then stretched out and pulled my hat over my eyes, and fell asleep.

I was waked up by feeling the toe of a boot in my ribs. It was only a touch, but the indignity was just as great as though my side had been smashed in. I opened my eyes and saw above me the face of a fellow named Sammy Went. It was a queer name that I've never blundered into since. Perhaps it was a nickname; I don't know.

Sammy Went was comparatively elderly. He must have been close to thirty and that made him next to Loomis in age. There is no good way to describe him unless you've seen something like him. He was just a scrawny runt with pimples all over his face so that he looked half raw, and he had a long under jaw and a recessive upper jaw, and his nose was long and crooked, and his eyes were bright pinheads under a slanted forehead. But nothing that I can say about Sammy Went will give you an idea of his repulsiveness.

He had only one talent in the world, but since that talent was wonderful skill with a revolver, he was at home with these crooks. He could not have kept a job even as a timekeeper in a grocery store, but he could kill his man every time, and that made all the difference.

Of all the men I met while I was with Loomis, he was the only one whose name meant anything to me. But I had heard of Sammy Went and his murders a good many times. Everybody in the West had, I suppose. Because he was one of those merciless fiends who will kill for the pleasure of killing. He had no more sense of honor, in a fight, than a hunting beast. Shooting from behind was as satisfactory to him as shooting from in front. It was simply the blood, the fall, and the dead body that he wanted to see.

The moment I saw him among the men of Loomis, I knew that the whole lot were rotten and that there was something worse than wrong with Loomis himself, for otherwise Sammy Went could not have been taken into the crowd.

Well, it was the ugly, leering face of Went that I saw above me, when I opened my eyes, and I knew that the hound was about to try his hand at bullying me.

He merely said: "The dishes ain't been washed. Hop to it, kid!" And he snapped the fingers of his famous right hand.

I hunched myself up on one elbow and looked around me. Everybody was watching me with a good deal of curiosity. Little Charlie stood agape with delight, plainly hoping that I might be humiliated, and plainly believing that I couldn't be downed by any mortal hand!

Well, I saw that my hopes of getting peacefully through the day were ruined. If I put up with this, every man in the outfit would kick me about. The suddenness of the shock washed all the blood out of my brain and made me see black, but I knew I had to say something, so I muttered:

"You whistle for your own dog. I don't belong to you!"

CHAPTER XVI

GUNS IN THE WOODS

WENT seemed a little surprised. He seemed a very great deal pleased, too. He stepped back, and said to the others: "He says that he ain't my dog. But maybe he's goin' to belong to me. A dead dog belongs to anybody that wants to claim the carcass. Maybe you're goin' to be a dead dog, Willis," he wound up, turning back to me.

I was pretty sick, and I was bewildered. Cold-blooded murder was what this devil had in mind, I knew. And even in a camp like this, I was surprised out of breath that such things could go on. Somehow, after what I had been through in merely rubbing elbows with Loomis, so to speak, and then in being almost savaged by Little Charlie, it seemed that I had endured about all that a fellow should have to go through. But now there was this thing, that was ten times worse.

I got up to one knee, saying: "I'll get my gun and come out to you, Went."

He just stood there and grinned, and kept on snapping the fingers of his right hand, and they were fleshless, and seemed to rattle like stones together.

I went in toward the cabin, while the rest of them stared.

I stumbled over a bump on the ground, and the whole crowd laughed. When I looked back, I could see Little Charlie as the single exception. He was shaking his great head until his ropy mustache swung from side to side and his hair shook out behind him.

Well, it wasn't the revolver that I had come for. It was the chance of being alone and getting my breath and rallying my smashed-up nerves. I fiddled around my pack for an instant, as though I were getting something out of it, and then I sat down—since there was nobody else in the long room—and held my head in my hands, and tried to think.

It seemed to me that I was there hardly an instant, with an express train of images shooting through my head—the Chief, Sue Carr, and above all a thousand scenes on the old ranch. If I could put my eye on the reality of that place for just one second, it seemed to me that enough strength would come out of it to restore me and make me able to go out there and fight like a man, even if I had to die, torn with lead bullets.

But I must have been a little while there in the room before a voice sang out close to me, and I saw the blond face and the savage eyes of Em shining at me from the door.

"He's in there holdin' this head! He's gone and turned yellow! He's yaller! He's yaller!" screamed Em, and went dancing away.

I could hear the dancing of his feet, and the Indian yell of glee from the rest of the pack. What a lot of cruel beasts they were, and how they snarled now over my bones, before I was dead!

Mostly I kept wondering what had happened to Loomis, that he should have disappeared so soon after arriving with me there. But on the whole, he would have been no help. He already had told me that when there was trouble in his camp, he believed in letting the boys fight the thing out among themselves.

Well, I got myself, somehow, to the door of the cabin, several times practicing the draw of my revolver on the way, and each time my fingers stumbled, as though they were numbed by the cold of a frosty morning. The air was warm enough, but the frost was in my spirit, all right.

When I got to the door of the cabin, I could see the whole gang of them doing a sort of a war dance, yelling, slapping each other on the back, and all laughing fit to die. Only Little Charlie, with his head down, was pulling at his thick mustache and trying to fit the new idea of me into the old one. But I couldn't see the man-killer, Went.

Then, off at the side, on the verge of the trees that came down closest to the cabin, I saw him sitting on a stump smoking a cigarette and grinning all over his deformed face.

Straight for him I started, and stumbled over the same little hummock of ground that had tripped me before. So that gave those beasts a chance to whoop again.

All my heart was for turning around and running for dear life, but my legs kept on taking me step after step nearer to Sammy Went. Then he stood up, and vanished among the trees; as though he were not sure enough of killing me in a simple fight in the open, but had to make it an Indian duel of hide-and-seek!

Well, his own murdering friends didn't like that very well, for they all screeched out at him to come into the open and let the rest of them enjoy the party that was to come. But Sammy didn't appear, and I found myself walking straight ahead among the trees, wondering when a bullet would strike me, the roar of the gun clapping against my ear an instant later.

The noise of the Loomis gang sounded rather far distant when a voice said behind me: "All right, you can take it here!"

I half turned, half made a motion to get my gun, and then saw that Sammy Went was standing there at the side, not six steps away, leaning one hand against a tree, and with the other covering me. No, he had taken no chances of making it a fair fight. I wondered why he had challenged me at all, but I suppose it was because on this occasion he wanted the bullet to enter me from in front. He would be able to brag, afterwards, that it was a fair fight. He could pull out my gun and leave it near my dead hand, and then let the others come and look at the remains of me.

I just looked at him for a minute, the way the sunlight fell in a splash across his hair and shoulders, and kindly left the ugliness of his face in shadow. The same sun made a golden pattern on the pine needles that covered the ground deeply. And I remember a squirrel frisking on a branch not far overhead, turning here and there, sitting up to scold, but never quite making up its mind that a noise would be a wise thing to make.

"What's the matter, Went?" I asked him, in a rusty, creaking sort of a voice. "I've never crossed you."

"No, you ain't," said Sammy Went, "but the minute that I seen you, I begun to wonder what you'd look like when facing a gun and, believe me, you look pretty yaller! But, besides, when you pass out, you might as well take the news along with you that Loomis didn't want you in the crowd. He just tipped me off to see how good you are, and now I'm goin' to see!"

Loomis! But if Loomis had not wanted me, what could have made him take me in the first place? Why had I been brought down here to be murdered quietly among the trees? And what did Loomis have against me in the first place?

These things went spinning blankly through my mind.

"Say one prayer," said Sammy Went, "and then get ready to take it. And fill your hand, you!"

When he started to speak, he was calm enough. But as the words went on, a spasm came over his face, and his voice went into a screech of devilish exultation, so that I had a picture of what a man is like when he's hungry for murder. And as he got to the words: "Fill your hand!" I knew that he was about to shoot.

There was no chance. I didn't even move my hand, but a revolver barked right behind me, almost in my ear. Sammy Went fired, too, and the bullet that smashed through his body only put his aim a little off its mark. Instead of braining me, that slug clipped the hat off my head and laid it neatly on the top of a little pine sapling behind me.

I didn't see that, at the time. I was simply staring at the way Sammy Went dropped his gun on the ground, as though marking the spot where he wanted to fall, and then dropped right over it with his head lying in the curl of one arm.

He had seemed a devil, an instant before. Now he

96

simply looked like a young lad asleep. After he hit the ground, he didn't so much as kick.

"You owe me one for that," said the voice of Ferrald, right at my ear.

I glanced back at him, and saw his gun and the satisfied grin on his face.

"And I owe *you* one, too," said he, "for bringing him inside shooting distance. Why, he's likely one of them that murdered Jerry. It warms me up, too, the way you faced him, kid. But you didn't have no chance. You're a man. You ain't used to the ways of snakes."

"Jim," I stammered, "I've got to get out of this. Loomis is against me. You heard what Sammy said."

"Get out of this? Throw up the game now that you've got everything working just right?" said Ferrald, sort of appalled, and gaping at me. "Maybe Loomis sort of changed his mind on the way to camp. Maybe you looked too honest, or something, to fit into his gang of thugs. But when he knows that you've killed Sammy Went, he'll feel different."

"But I didn't kill Sammy," said I.

"Shake a slug out of your gun," said Ferrald.

I did that, and he threw his own empty cartridge on the ground, and took the loaded one from me. I understood then. It would look as though I had shot Sammy in a fair fight. I started to protest, but Ferrald whispered rapidly:

"They're coming. Stand your ground. Don't back up an inch. Make a cigarette. Start reloading your Colt. Be smoking. Sit down on that log. You're doin' fine. And this'll give you a name among 'em. If you don't run, Loomis won't suspect you know nothin'. And we got him in our hands. When the Chief comes, we got 'em all in our hands!"

He faded away. I thought of bolting into the brush, rather than mixing with the devils that I heard crashing through the bushes toward me. But then I could see that, if I ran for it without a horse, they'd soon be chasing me, and they'd soon have me, too. So I just sat down on a log, as Ferrald had told me to do, and lighted a smoke, and I had finished reloading my gun at the minute that Little Charlie came busting through into the clearing.

When he saw Sammy Went lying on his face, he threw up both hands and let out a whoop that blew like a trumpet through my ears.

"He's beat Sammy! He's beat Sammy! I knew he would!" thundered Little Charlie.

The others came through on the run, after Charlie. Seven or eight men were pretty soon swarming around, and I think it was Em who lifted Sammy Went and turned him on his back.

"That's old-school shooting," said one of them. "Look! He aimed for the button of his coat, and he smashed the button, too!"

One of the others picked up my hat and looked at the holes in it. He whistled and passed the hat around.

Oh, Sammy Went was dead, all right. He was dead as a doornail, and it was true that the bullet had hit a button on his coat before it slid through the life of Sammy and dropped him into the long darkness.

Emory came and asked me for a look at my gun, and after he'd examined the way it was fixed, he gave it back to me, and said:

"I guess we been a pack of fools."

It seemed to me that a few words were necessary. Unless I said them, these people would be ready to jump at me any time.

I merely said: "You fellows are a pretty tough lot. I've been with some hard crowds before, but I've never been where they give you an initiation ceremony like this."

Then I went on to do some plain lying, and said: "I didn't want to kill Sammy. But you see where he dropped. He tried to get me from the side, by surprise, and I just had to shoot at the shadow of him out of the corner of my eye—the shadow and the flash of a button on his coat. I wouldn't have aimed to bump him off; I would have just smashed his arm for him, or something like that."

CHAPTER XVII

A CHANGE OF LUCK

THAT was a lie which paid dividends, at least for a time. I didn't feel so very sneaking about telling it, either, though perhaps some of you may think that I deserved what was coming to me later on, because I'd talked like that. But I felt that I had to use every card that was in my hand, and impose on these thugs as well as I could.

Every man jack of them looked on me with curious eyes, and they glanced at one another after I had finished. But they all took me mighty seriously and seemed to think that I *did* regret killing that scavenging coyote of a Sammy Went, and that I would have aimed to brush him out of the way by nudging him with a chunk of lead. They seemed to think that I *did* consider this a mere initiation ceremony, and that I admired them for being so tough!

But nobody was pleased, compared with Charlie Little. He went around laughing and rubbing his hands together, and now and then he fetched a whack at one of the crooks, and they dodged for fear of having their backs broken. He was delighted, you see, because the death of Sammy Went seemed to indicate that I *was* a desperate character, and that made his own beating a comparatively simple thing. He let the others carry the dead body out from the trees into the open, and he walked along with his huge arm thrown over my shoulders, and he kept shouting and roaring with his pleasure.

"He ain't so big, but there's something to him!" he would roar. "You ain't so much to look at, kid, but you look good to me. They ain't goin' to kick this wild cat around, no more. They ain't goin' to kick you, kid. And the next one that tries, I'll save you some of your chores by breakin' him up for you!"

When the body was brought into the clearing near

the cabin, it was laid down near the low hummock that I had tripped over twice before.

"We might as well bury him right here beside Jake," said Em, and I realized that I had been stumbling over a grave!

Some of them thought that he ought to be kept until Loomis returned, but Em said:

"Why for? Would Loomis like to see him? Is he any prettier dead than he was livin' ?"

Four of them set to work digging, right away, and in an hour they had scooped out a grave. Then they got the dead body ready for burial. It was a very simple procedure. They simply went through his clothes and took his wallet, which had several hundred dollars in it—the proceeds would be given to the first man who was seriously wounded in a raid, it appeared—and they put with the wallet a diamond stickpin. A gold Mexican charm was about to be taken, too, but one of the men said that a fellow like Sammy Went ought to take all the luck he could get hold of along with him. They left his guns on him, too, and the cook got down into the grave, at the last moment, and put a bandanna of his over the face of Sammy.

He merely said, as he dragged his crippled body out of the grave again: "I wouldn't want even Sammy to have dirt in his eyes."

That was the end of the ceremony. I stood by, feeling a little sick, and watched the earth being shoveled back on top of the dead man. Nobody could be very sorry that a fellow like Sammy had gone to his last accounting, but still he was a human being, and I felt a certain amount of pity for him. The mound that remained when the earth was heaped over was trampled down by all hands, and I noticed that every one of the boys took his turn for a moment in stamping on the grave, even if it were to leave only a single print of his boot on the top of it.

The cook was called any of three names: "Ray," or "Sting," or "Sting Ray." He seemed to be the most sentimental fellow in the crowd, in spite of his sour face and ways, for when the ceremony was finished, he brought out a couple of buckets of water and threw them over the grave mound, muttering something about starting the grass to grow as soon as possible.

Well, take it all in all, it was a queer moment for me, but never so strange as the short time that followed when these people said what they thought about such things as immortality of the soul and the life after death.

They all, strange to say, were assured that there was some sort of a future life. One of them said: "Everything can't stop happening all in a bunch."

Another one had the idea that there was always something in what a lot of people believed.

"Where there's smoke, there's fire," he said.

"A fine hot, clear blaze you're goin' to find," said Sting Ray.

"Maybe I am," said the other man. "But nothing to what you'll have laid out for you."

"That's right," agreed Sting Ray, nodding his gloomy head. "I'll catch a good hot part, all right. They'll work forced draft on the furnaces when they hear that Sting Ray is coming down."

"That reminds me of a story," said Little Charlie.

Every one called for the story, and he went on:

"There was a gent by the name of Holy Joe Twitcher, down in Arizona. Any of you boys know him?"

None of them knew "Holy Joe" and Little Charlie went on:

"They called him Holy Joe because nobody could ever see nothing holy about him. He'd gone and married himself a squaw and got himself about a dozen half-breeds, and the oldest son was a monkey-faced brat the size of a chipmunk and the nacher of a snake. And Holy Joe, he gets himself all boiled, one day, and into a fight with a greaser, and the greaser runs a knife into Joe, and Joe takes and beats in the head of the greaser with the butt of his gun, after shootin' all the bullets and hittin' nothing but the walls and the ceiling.

"Well, there was a lot of blood in Holy Joe, but most of it had run out of him, and you couldn't pour in enough whisky to warm him up none, and make him feel good. One of the boys sashayed out to Joe's place and told the family that he was dying. But nobody cared much, and the squaw said that life was goin' to be pretty easy, now that her old man was out of the way, because she said that he made her more work than all the kids put together. And the kids, they didn't show much sorrow, neither, because Joe had done nothin' but kick them around.

"But the monkey-faced one, the oldest of the batch, roped a pony and rode into town, and sat down on the floor of the saloon, beside where his old man was dying. Joe cussed him a little and didn't seem glad to see him, and kept saying that he felt mighty cold, and would somebody put more clothes on him? And they kept on piling blankets and things on Joe, but still they couldn't warm him up none with wool or with whisky.

"Pretty soon Joe groans out that he's goin' to die, that he's dyin' right then, and he wants to see a minister. Which surprises us all, because we never seen Joe do nothin' about a church except to shoot the windows out of one. Joe says for somebody to go, and to go fast. And then the monkey-faced brat pipes up and says to take our time, because his old man ain't near dead, yet.

" 'Why ain't I near dead, you little blankety-blank son of a blankety coyote?' says Holy Joe.

" 'Because,' says the kid, 'when you get nigh onto dyin', you'll begin to feel the heat, and you'll throw off these here blankets before you get that close to hell.'

"Them of us that was standing around laughed a good bit at this here remark," went on Little Charlie, when the chuckling had died off, "but the funny thing was that in the end Holy Joe *did* throw off all the blankets and stuff and he sung out for 'Air, air!' a couple of times, before he passed in his chips."

This story told by Little Charlie seemed enough to bridge the gap between the death of Sammy Went and ordinary pursuits. A blanket was rolled out on the grass, and half a dozen of them sat down cross-legged to a game of poker. Some of the others went off to see the cook ride a new horse he had added to his string.

I went with that batch, and I give you my word that I never saw a finer bit of riding. Bullets had broken up Sting Ray, but horses had helped to smash him, and still he loved to take his chances with a wild-caught mustang, like the one he was gentling now. For twenty minutes, that broncho kept exploding without a stop, and finally it was beaten and stood with its head hanging and the blood trickling down from its nose. Sting Ray got off, more dead than alive, and went staggering like a drunk back toward the house. I heard that every day for a week he'd been riding that mustang to a fare-you-well, and every day there was the same ending, and still the devil was just as bright and strong in that mustang the next time that Sting climbed into the saddle.

We were wearing out the afternoon like this, when Loomis came back, and with him there was a stranger and the girl, Sue Carr. I saw them at a distance, and I knew it was she by the lilt of her in the saddle, because nobody that ever lived had quite her way in the saddle.

I peered around the back of the house, where I was shaving, and saw the three of them coming, and I hurried up to finish washing off the suds.

The Sting Ray, who was working over the fixing of some venison steaks, asked: "Who's coming?"

"Loomis," said I, "and Sue Carr, and somebody else so far away that I can't make out his face."

"But you know the girl, eh?" said Sting Ray, giving me a glint of his eye.

The heat came into my face before I could very well turn away.

"Listen, kid," Sting Ray said. "There ain't many of us that ain't dizzy about her, but she belongs to Loomis. Don't you go and forget that. You're a handy bird with a gun, or you wouldn't 'a' bumped off Sammy Went, but you wouldn't have a chance agin' Loomis. Know that?"

"Sure I know that," said I. "I'm not such a fool."

"Nobody has any chance agin' him," said Sting Ray, "excepting one gent in the world, and *he's* been three years in jail, to slow up his gun hand and dull his eye."

It gave me a good big thrill, you can imagine, to hear a hardy fellow like Sting Ray talk in this way about the Chief. Then the sadness came back over me when I thought of what the Chief had been, and of what he was right now.

I got myself ready and went around to the front of the house just as Loomis was demanding what was the meaning of the new grave. Little Charlie did the speaking. I heard his words out of the corner of my mind, so to speak, while I put my eyes on the girl until she turned and gave me one bright, meaning look over her shoulder.

The man who had ridden down with Loomis I could not make out, except that he had a head of bright-red hair almost as flame-colored as mine, and that there was something familiar about his big head and chunky, short body.

In the meantime, while my heart did a toe dance because Sue was so near, Little Charlie was sketching in the fight between me and Sammy Went, and he put in a lot of details that never had happened. It was enough, anyway, to do justice to everything except Ferrald. He made me out a fire-breathing monster, all right, and just as he got to the burying scene, the new man who had come down with Loomis turned around. I recognized the face of Johnny Dill, a fellow who had been to school with me, and a regular bad one from the word go.

When Johnny saw me, he snaked out a gun and covered me, and yelled:

"He ain't Dick Willis! His name is Rickie Willard, and he's a brother of the Chief! Look out, all of you! He's tryin' to double-cross you! He's the brother of the Chief!"

The ground sort of opened under me. The sky sort of came down hot and close over my head. I thought I had been playing a winning hand, and now luck struck me straight in the face!

104

CHAPTER XVIII

A STORM

THERE was not the slightest chance of resisting. Even in darkness I could not have got away, I guess, because the name of the Chief had turned all of those fellows into hunting cats. It frightened them so much just to hear that word that, even as they covered me with their guns and came sneaking toward me, they flashed glances over their shoulders toward the woods, as if they expected the Chief himself to come charging out at them. And if he *had* come charging just then, I've half an idea that the gang of them would have scattered like birds, with the exception of Loomis.

And even Loomis was not so steady, I can tell you!

He called out to me to stick up my hands, but I'd been through so much that I was more disgusted than afraid, it seemed.

"Because my real name's Rickie Willard, instead of Dick Willis, why should I stick up my hands?" said I.

Loomis came right up and rested the muzzle of his gun in the small of my back.

"Because," he said, "there's plenty of poison in even a small rattlesnake! Put up your hands. Charlie, fan him. No; somebody else do the job. Em, come and go through him! Charlie's lost his head about this fellow. He loves him because he likes the hand that can beat him, I suppose."

Emory fanned me, and got my gun and knife, and a few odds and ends. There was nothing of importance.

Out of the whirl of my mind, I looked for Sue, but I couldn't find her. Somebody brought out a pair of handcuffs that I learned later had once been fitted over the wrists of Loomis. It always amazed me to think of a sheriff who would be fool enough to put Loomis in irons instead of shooting him on the spot. That poor sheriff got a bullet through the head for taking the odd chance. That was his reward for playing the game in the right way! Anyway, those handcuffs fitted me to a *t*. They took me into the cabin, and Loomis told the rest that they could scatter. He wanted to be alone with me.

The men went out, and I heard Emory say:

"You can't go in, Sue. Loomis wants to be alone with him."

"No; come along in," said Loomis quickly.

Sue came in and sauntered across the room, and she stood across the table from where I was sitting with my elbows resting on the edge of it.

"That's why the little badger is so game, eh?" said she to Loomis. "Got the blood of the Chief in him, has he?"

"That's why you like him so much?" said Loomis.

He said it in a certain way that gave me a start and made the girl turn sharply on him, also.

"In what way?" she demanded.

"In a way that makes you want to belong to him!" said Loomis through his teeth.

Suddenly I remembered the form of a man that I had seen disappearing through a second-story window, the night before—a figure that had climbed like a cat. Why, it was Loomis, of course! He had been outside of one of the windows, spying, during the time that the girl and her father and I were there alone.

What part of the talk had he heard? If not the talk, how many gestures?

In any case, if I had been a dead man before, I was doubly dead if he knew that she was fond of me. But his face made no change, except for what seemed to me an added shining of his eyes.

He just sat there and looked from the girl to me.

I couldn't speak. There was nothing for me to say. But Sue? Why, she broke out into the pleasantest laughter that you ever heard, and she said:

"Harry, Harry, are you enough of an idiot to think that I give a rap about this bull-faced pup?"

106

I blinked at her. I saw Loomis take a deep breath, too.

Then she flew into a passion and cried out at him: "You come spying on me, do you, when I'm doing dirty work in order to pump your new man, and try to find out who he is and why he's up in the mountains? And while I'm doing my best for you, you sneak around and spy on me, do you?"

Loomis stood up from the table. As for me, I went sick all over. I slumped down in the chair and covered my face with my hands. I couldn't stand it, because I loved her, and as she talked, I could remember how extremely casual she had been, and how she had asked me those questions about myself!

"I almost believe you, Sue," said he, muttering.

"I don't care what you believe," she raged at him. "I don't care what you do, either. To be spied on, sneaked after, watched like a cat! It's all you are—a cat—a wild cat—a bloodthirsty wild cat, and I'm through with you!"

She started for the door. He blocked her way, with both of his arms extended, and backed up before her.

"Will you wait one minute, Sue?" he asked.

"Not a minute—not a half a minute!" she cried. "I'm walking out of here once and for all. And when you ride our way, forget that there's a house by the lake. You're not welcome!"

He still blocked her.

"I only want to say that I believe you, Sue," said he. "But last night it seemed to me that something went between the pair of you—that there was something in your eyes when you looked at one another."

"There was," she said. "There was calf love in his eyes, and a lot of interest in mine, because I knew that he was something besides what he pretended. And you—you came down to spy when I was trying to find out—"

"I was a suspicious fool!" said he. "Forgive me, Sue."

"And that was why you brought him down here today?" she asked him, stepping back and looking at him with a sneer. "You simply wanted to brush him out of the way, did you? You simply passed the word to Mr. Murderer Went to slaughter him. Why, no matter whose brother he is, I should think that you'd be sick with shame, Harry. *I'm* sick about you, at least!"

He got hold of one of her hands. I was watching them, out of a gray haze, miserable.

Still that face of his could show no emotion, but he was saying: "I'll get down on my knees and beg you to pardon me, Sue. If that will do any good, I'll get down on my knees!"

He meant it, too. I could see that he really would abase himself like that, and I understood that she must mean more to him than even his savage name among men.

The girl was a bit impressed by what he said, too, or by his manner of saying it. She said: "Drop my hand!"

He dropped it like a shot. She stepped back and went on:

"I don't know what to think. It's not a matter of forgiveness, either. It's a matter of thinking. What *am* I to think of you?"

"That I'm a poor, desperate fellow who loves you, Sue," said he, "and that you've driven me half crazy, because I really thought that you were losing your head about him!"

"Losing my head?" she cried. "You *are* crazy, Harry, if you think that I could lose my head about a thing like that! Look at him!"

He did turn, at that, and looked me over, and he sighed again, with relief.

"I'm sorry," said Loomis weakly.

"Are you?" said the girl.

She stepped up to the table and went on fiercely, with all the savage in her blazing out at her eyes as she said:

"Look at him—the poor, stupid, flat-faced nothing! And ask me if I'd do more than make a fool of him? And *what* a fool! I meet him in the afternoon—and in the evening I make him think that I'm out of my mind about him. How? By letting him hold my hand for ten seconds!

108

And yet you think that I've lost my head about such a creature as this?"

Every word was burning acid that went through my skin and got at my vital soul and consumed it to ashes. But, after all, as I stared at her, I saw what a folly it had been, that happy hope of mine, and the more she raged at Loomis in her pride and in her anger, the more I could see the continents that separated her beauty from such a "creature" as myself. I almost lost some of my grief, admiring the flash of her eyes, and the swift, strong gestures, and the ring of her voice.

"I've been wrong in every way. I see what a fool I am. I'll always be a fool—until I'm safely married to you, Sue!"

"And then to bring him down here and hand him over to your murderer to get rid of him!"

"Sue," said Loomis, "do you think that I'm afraid of him? I'll take him out this moment and give him an even break—"

"Ah, bah, bah!" she cried. "You talk of an even break when you have all of your men around, and he's by himself, and his nerves smashed. Look at the white of his face! And now you're going to play the gallant hero? I tell you, Harry, I almost begin to doubt your nerve!"

He made a turn up and down the room. Then he threw out a hand toward her.

"Tell me what you want me to do with him!" he exclaimed. "You can't ask me to turn him loose, to bring the Chief and his crowd down on us here!"

"What do I care what you do with him?" she answered. "Do what you please. Take him out and cut his throat like a stuck pig. That's probably what you'll do. You're so afraid of the Chief that even his little pug-nosed brother makes the whole crew of you tremble. I saw what happened when the name was used, a minute ago. And I was ashamed that there should be such men in the world —such yellow cowards! Why did I ever look at you?— that's what I don't know! I thought you were a gallant, unhappy, desperate sort of a man with something noble hidden in you, and now—now I look down into the truth! And I'm sick!"

"Sue," said he, keeping his voice level, though he was badly shaken, as I could see. "You stay in here a little while, will you please? Don't go storming away like this. Take a few minutes and try to get yourself together, Sue. You can't go away, leaving nothing but words like these behind. Stay here, please. I'll go out. In five minutes I'll come back. Just remember, while I'm gone, that I feel like dust under your feet. If you'll give me a chance, I'll try to build myself back into something worth thinking about."

He backed toward the door.

"Will you take me out, too?" I asked him.

"You?" said he.

"Am I to stay here while she sharpens her claws on me?" I demanded grimly.

"The devil with you and what you want!" said he, and disappeared through the doorway. As he went, the girl began to walk up and down the room, but as she walked past the table she said in a low voice:

"I've seen the Chief. He wants to get to you. I came to bring you the message. What can we do?"

CHAPTER XIX

A TALK WITH LOOMIS

WELL, I sat like a dummy, more than a man. All of my world had been turned upside down, and now it was set right side up again. And here she was walking up and down to help cover the sound of her low-pitched voice and to make Loomis, if he were anywhere near, think that she was still in a towering rage.

But I could only gradually drag myself back out of darkness and begin to see the light again. She had said things that went through me just like bullets, and the misery I had felt could not be cured at one touch.

Vaguely, too, the great news came rushing through my mind—the Chief in the Blue Water Mountains, the Chief looking for me, the Chief on my trail, no matter what weakness might be in him!

"I don't know," I muttered. "I can't think. I'm bewildered, Sue."

"Try, try!" she said. "Think of something that must be done. Could you break away, if I managed to set your hands free? Could you get to my horse, just outside the cabin, and bolt away? She goes just like the wind. They'd never catch you."

"Not with horses, but they'd tag me with bullets, easily enough," I told her.

She wrung her hands together.

"The Chief and father, they'll work together," she said. "They'll get men together—"

Then she stopped herself short and moaned: "It's no good. The moment riders came, no matter how they sneaked through the dark, they'd be found out, and the first thing that the Loomis men would do before they started fighting or running would be to murder you. Oh, Dick, what—what can I do?"

My brain was still buzzing, as I thought over the dynamo and the brain that was always working inside her. And still I couldn't believe, with all my might, that really she felt this way about me, and didn't call me, in her heart of hearts, a "bull-faced pup."

You see, I was still staggered and reeling from the blows that I had received.

Then she was saying: "Is there no way that you can be taken out of here right now, by me? If I got in front of you, they wouldn't shoot, I think. Could we try that?"

I shook my head.

As she went on walking, I said to her:

"You've done all that you can do. It's not very likely, now, that he'll have me shot down in a hurry. He'll wait a day or two, anyway. Unless there's some sort of alarm that scares the flock of them away from the place. In that case, he'll make pretty short work of me. But, in the meantime, he's going to remember some of the things you said to him."

"I'll find a way," she said rapidly. "I'll find a way. Heaven will show me some way. Oh, Dick, why didn't you tell me, last night, about the Chief? I never would have let you take the chance of coming here with Loomis!"

"I had to come," I said. "There's more than I can explain. Only, if you see the Chief, tell him that I'm here because I want to be here, and tell him that everything's all right."

Suddenly tears burst out of her eyes. She was at the wall, leaning against it, weeping into her hands, when the great Loomis reappeared.

He took one glance at her, and a great breath of relief came out from him. He hurried over to her and touched her shoulder.

"Sue," he said, "I'm sorry. I'm on my knees to you. Forgive me!"

"Don't touch me!" she gasped.

There was no acting in that. No actress can make her whole body shudder in such a way.

He stepped back and shook his head, and stared at her, because it was apparent that he considered that the tears were on his account and indicated the ending of the storm.

He walked around her in a singularly furtive, helpless way, and finally he said:

"Please stop crying, Sue. I'm not worth it. But if you care that much about me, if you care enough to cry from disappointment, maybe I can make you laugh, some day, with happiness. Even when I hoped you liked me, I never guessed that you could care about any one as much as this. I never dreamed that anything in the world could make you cry, my dear."

She got her eyes dry, at last, and turned slowly around. He made a gesture toward her with both arms, but she put her hand up and stopped him. She leaned for a minute against the wall, looking weak and very ill.

"It's all right, Harry," she said. "Just let me get out of

112

here, please. I want to go home. I want to go alone."

"I'll take you. I don't want you to be alone."

"It's what you want that counts!" she said bitterly. "I'm not able to have a wish—not even a wish to be alone."

"I'll ride half a mile behind you, if you wish," said he.

"I don't want you."

"Then I'll let you go alone," said Loomis. "But that's dangerous, Sue. There are people in these mountains—"

"I know," she said in weary disgust. "There are people in these mountains who throw a poor, stupid, silly fellow into irons until they can think of a pleasant way of cutting him up! I have to go!"

He stood back from her with a good deal of dignity, saying: "Does it mean that I'm not to see you again—ever?"

"I don't know," she said. "I don't know anything. I have to think. I'm half crazy, Harry! And my heart's breaking in me! Just let me go—and let me be alone."

He let her go, at that, and she passed out through the door, while he watched her from the threshold.

When he turned around, he had a lighted face. He was in such a passion of joy that he walked up and down the room and struck his right fist into the palm of his left hand, over and over again. And sometimes he threw back his head and drew in a great breath. But, even in the midst of this transport, I give you my word that his facial expression hardly changed at all, except for a ghost of a smile that came about his mouth, from time to time.

Finally he came over to the table and touched the tips of his fingers to it. I looked up at him with my dazed eyes, wondering, still, at the skill with which she had made him think that all of her emotion was on his account. And still I was tasting and retasting all her beauty, and still her voice went breathlessly and sweetly through me, like a wind out of paradise.

"I'm sorry for you, Rickie, if that's what people call you," he said.

"Aye," said I, "or Stubby, or Shorty, or Red. Almost any name is good enough for me."

A flash of his twisted smile appeared on his face.

"And you thought that she really had lost her head about you, eh?" he asked me. "You poor devil!"

"You thought the same thing," said I. "Remember that!"

"I was a fool," he admitted. "And she could make a fool out of anybody. But you saw how she loves me, boy! You saw how she was torn to pieces because I had disappointed her? I don't know what put her expectations of me so high. But there they are! In the clouds!"

He made a gesture above his head, and began to walk up and down the room again, because he was hardly able to contain himself.

Still the flare of joy came blazing up in his eyes, again and again, and still he struck his hands together.

Finally, however, he came back and took a chair opposite me.

"Well," he said, "we'll talk about you."

"I don't want to talk," said I.

"I tell you," said he in his calm voice, "that I'm really half sorry for you. She's torn you to bits, I know. But get over that. She's not for *you*, Rickie—if that's your name."

"She's outside of my class," I agreed. "But think of her lying to me, softening her eyes for me, loving me with the way she looked at me! Think of what a crook she is!"

"Because she loves Loomis," said he. "And *Loomis* happens to be a crook. And because she was made for me! That's the reason. Because the little fox was going to use her wits to find out about you, for me, and it's a wonder that she didn't tear all of your secrets out of you in half a minute! If I'd given her another day, she would have managed it, all right. I'll never suspect her again!"

He struck the table with his fist.

Then he went on: "Talk frankly with me, Rickie, and perhaps I can see a way out this mess for you. Come out with everything. Put the truth on the table, and I'll see what I can do. The girl thinks that you've gotten into

114

trouble on her account and that her hands will be dirty if anything happens to you. That's why I'm wasting any time at all on a Willard. But go ahead, and we'll see."

Tell him the truth? Tell him that the Chief had lost his nerve, and that that werewolf, Ferrald, was waiting in the woods, and that I was there for the sake of trying to do my part in ruining the gang?

No, I could not say that; but I thought of a convenient system of lies.

"Loomis," I said, "look me in the eye and tell me if you think I'm fool enough to try to lie to you?"

"I don't know," said Loomis, doing exactly as I said, and boring into me with the gray of his eyes. "I don't know. I hope you're not going to try it."

"Let me tell you," said I, "that when I came sashaying up here into the mountains, it was all on account of the Chief."

Loomis started.

"Ah? He sent you ahead to spy out the lay of the land, did he?"

"He's through with crooked business, if that's what you mean," said I.

"Once a crook, always a crook," replied Loomis.

"Have it your own way," said I. "But after he came home, when I told him that I wanted to get at some of the easy money, he told me to forget it. He said he preferred money he worked for. It might cost you more sweat, but you didn't pay for it with so much jail, and he said that one day in jail was worse than one month of punching cows."

"Did he say that?" asked Loomis.

"Yes."

"He *might* say that," murmured Loomis, "because he's such a high-strung, high-nerved sort of a bird. He hated the jail, eh? But what brought you up here?"

"Well, if he wouldn't come, I decided that I'd go by myself and see what I could find. And I found something, all right! I found that, just because I happened to be the brother of the Chief, my name was mud, and everybody had a gun ready for me, and even the pretty girls, they make a fool of me and play against me. That's what I've found, and finally I've got my hands into irons, and here I sit till Mr. Loomis gets ready to chew me up. And why?—I wanta know.

"Because I smiled at a pretty girl? Is that reason enough? Or because I killed Sammy Went, that was after my scalp? Is it my fault that my name is Willard? Have I got any cause to go around fighting for the Chief? How much did he ever work on the ranch? Why did he leave it on my hands for ten years? And yet I'm to be bumped off because he's my brother! A rotten run of luck, I call it!"

Loomis looked at me without blinking for a full five minutes.

Then he said: "The jury's out on you. We'll get the verdict a bit later."

He said it just like that, and got up and left the cabin.

CHAPTER XX

THE CHIEF'S ARRIVAL

THE rest of that evening, that night, and the next morning, the "jury remained out." I had the feeling at any time, during those long hours, that the decision might be taken against me, and that I would get a bullet through the brain and an even quicker burial than that which had been granted to Sammy Went.

One thing that saved me, I'm sure, was the curiosity of the gang about my brother. They spent nearly every waking moment asking me about the Chief, because to several of them he was no more than a legend, and even those who had known him, and actually seen him in action, wanted to have their own impressions brightened.

I could tell, by watching their faces—even the immobile face of Loomis—that they were prepared to believe almost anything about the Chief. So I drew a long bow and kept arrows in the air, so to speak.

I told them about everything that had any basis of fact, such as his horse breaking and his rifle and revolver shooting, and I went right on and made him into a man of mystery. I took a melancholy pleasure in talking like this, because I knew that the Chief was no longer the miracle man that they thought him to be, and that I had always grown up feeling him to be. The hand of the law had crushed the heart out of his old self. And so, in a sense, I was glorifying a dead man, and there was a bitter pleasure in that.

It was amusing to me, in a grim way, to see Loomis sitting with his face resting on one hand, while he stared at me and devoured the stories of the Chief that I told him.

That night I slept with an extra pair of the irons on my legs. There were several sets of manacles in the place, and they had all been fitted on Loomis, at one time or another. He was proud of them in a rather childish way.

Nobody sat up to keep guard over me, because I had simply been put up in an attic room with a flimsy board flooring, so that if I stepped on it the creaking would wake up the people beneath. Besides, the rattling of my chains would be enough to rouse them.

I lay awake for a time devising ways of muffling the chains with my clothes, and then twisting up the bedding to make a rope, and *rolling* slowly across the floor, so that my distributed weight would have less chance of making the floor boards groan.

But if I tried to drop out of that window, which opened at the end of the room, there was a drop of nearly a hundred feet to the ground. For there was a rim of rock, just at this side of the house, which seemed to have been left there by the glacier plow that once had remodeled all of these mountains. And how could I make a rope of bed-clothes long enough to cover this distance?

I went to sleep still fumbling at the problem with a weary brain. When I awakened, it was well past sunup, for the golden light of the early sun was pouring through the window and making a big splotch of color on the slanting ceiling. Emory was standing with his head and shoulders above the level of the trapdoor that opened on the ladder which communicated with the big room beneath.

He was saying: "Wake up, Rickie. There's news, and big news. The Chief is after you!"

That got me out of the bed and down that ladder as quickly and lightly as though the chains were made of feathers. When I got to the lower floor, all the rest of the gang were up except young Dill, who had betrayed me. He was sitting up with the blanket sliding off him, and yawning so that all his yellow teeth showed.

Loomis, with a cigarette between his lips already, was standing in the center of the room talking to a big, shaggy bear of a man whom I had not seen before. Now Loomis said:

"Well, tell them all over again just what you told me, Nat."

Nat turned to the lot of us and said: "Well, I was ridin' around and takin' a slant at everything, and wonderin' when the cold of the night would let up, when I seen a thin rise of smoke out of a patch of trees on the far side of the lake. So I rode around to that side, and the firelight was still stronger than the morning light, and it was by the fire that I seen a big blaze had been sliced off the face of a tree that the fire was built under. And on the white of the wood there was wrote like this:

" 'LOOMIS: I want to talk with you about ransoming my brother. If you'll agree to let me come in peace, I'll work my way up to within talking distance of your house, through the trees. If you agree to the truce, build a small fire in front of your house, and I'll come in.'

"I wrote that down on an envelope, and brought it in. 'Willard,' it is signed."

The sleep was wiped out of every eye by this yarn, I

118

can tell you. As for me, the lightnings started jumping across my brain. Because I wondered how the Chief, poor wreck that he was, could have possibly worked up his nerve far enough to make him risk the danger of approaching as close as that to the house.

The gang held a conclave on the spot, as though it didn't matter what I heard of their mean ideas.

Most of those crooks were for building the fire and then scattering scouts through the trees to shoot down the Chief as he came in, and I must say that it seemed the logical plan to me, for a gang without any decent sense of honor.

But Loomis vetoed the idea. He said: "We're dealing with a man who can tell trouble while it's still behind a mountain. You're not wild Indians, though you *think* you are. But I'll tell you what would happen. As he came in, he'd spot one of you smart lads scouting him, and he'd hunt the hunter, and put a knife in his back, and then ride away, leaving the bad news behind him. No; if we want to get hold of him, we'll have to play a better game than that, and pretend to play it honestly. Build a fire, one of you, and put on plenty of green leaves to make the smoke he can see. Afterward, we'll figure out what to do."

Little Charlie was cook for the day; Dill was the roustabout. Between them they cooked breakfast of bacon, pone, and coffee. I sat in a corner from which I could look out the door and see the smoke rising from the fire. I tried to choke down some food, but I could hardly swallow, because excitement and fear were closing up my throat. I could see past the fire to the brightness of the lake in the morning sun, and how the green shadows of the trees stretched across the face of the lake. But the others had time to get through their breakfast and their first cigarettes after it, while still they put their heads together and confabbed.

The sun was well up the sky, and I had made up my mind that the Chief would never come, when a great mellow-ringing voice broke out from the trees nearest to the house, crying:

"Loomis! Harry Loomis!"

There were three windows on the long side of the bunk room, facing toward those trees, and instantly there was a pair of rifles at each of the windows, and careful eyes peering out. Loomis had arranged all of that. He himself stood out of view of the trees beside the door, and whooped out the answer:

"Hello—Chief?"

"Yes, I'm here to talk to you, Loomis. Come out and have a chat."

Somehow, it heartened me to hear the voice of my brother. I could almost forget that he had changed to a weak shadow of his old self. The big, honest, musical sound of his voice reassured me and warmed my heart.

But Loomis was laughing.

"I'm not such a fool, Chief!" he called.

"What sort of ransom do you want?" shouted the Chief.

His voice seemed to be coming nearer, as one got used to hearing it.

Loomis answered:

"I'm sending out a man to talk to you. He'll let you know."

He turned around to me, and said:

"Stand up!"

I stood up.

"You're going to walk out there the way you are," said he. "You're going to step up to those trees, and remember that we've got you covered every minute with our guns, and if you try to make a quick dive to get to cover, you'll hit the ground dead before you get out of sight. Understand?"

I ran my eyes over the line of guns and the faces behind the guns, and I nodded. "I understand, all right," said I. For every one of those men was an expert rifleman.

"Very well," said Loomis; "you'll be standing out there in the open air, but you'll be less free than you are here inside this room, among us!"

120

"Yes," said I, nodding. "I can see that."

"When you get out there," said Loomis, "you'll stop close to the trees, when I call to you to halt. And then you're going to tell your brother that, unless he agrees to give himself up for you, you'll be a dead man before noon. And if he does give himself up, you're safe. Go out and talk to him!"

I managed to make a cigarette with my hands, in spite of the irons dangling and jangling. I was smoking it and inhaling deep as I walked out through the doorway and headed for the trees, where they advanced a long, wedge-shaped point in the direction of the house.

I must have walked like a cat on wet ground, because every moment I felt as though bullets would begin to tear into me from the cabin. However, I was almost at the verge of the trees before Loomis yelled: "Halt!"

I stopped short, banging my heels together like a soldier, because I knew that it was quick death to pretend not to hear him. He was taking his chance, too, because the shelter of the brush was only a few steps away from me.

Then Loomis thundered behind me: "There he is, Chief. He'll tell you that if you want him free, money ransom won't interest us. But we'll turn him loose if you'll give yourself up in his place!"

Something rustled behind the outer screen of the leaves, but I could see nothing. For, of course, the Chief didn't dare to show himself to me for fear that the rifles in the house would spot him, also, and blow him to bits. Then the voice of the Chief came out to me, softly:

"Rickie, why did you do it? Why did you do it?"

"It was just one step after another, Chief," I told him. "I hadn't planned things. But there were happenings that brought me here. That's all I can say. I didn't want to get you into trouble. I wanted to keep you out of it!"

"I'm going to go in and take your place," he told me. "I'm just saying good-by to the world, for a minute. Just a minute, Rickie!"

"Chief," I gasped at him, "don't talk like a fool!

They'll kill you by inches. They'll tear you to pieces. There's not a one of them that isn't afraid of you, and people that are scared are always cruel!"

"I'm making up my mind," said his shaking voice. "I'm—I'm coming out. I'm going to save you, Rickie. Trust to me. I'll—I'll be there right away!"

Well, when he said that, I stopped worrying about the danger of him throwing himself away for me, because I was sure that, if he could not nerve himself right in the beginning to step out, and face the rifles of the house, and face the worse sort of a death that would be waiting for him if he were allowed to come inside of the house— if he could not make that step in the beginning, he would never be able to make it later on. Because every instant the poor bits of courage that were left to him were oozing out. I could thank Heaven for only one thing—that I could not see his face as the struggle worked in it.

CHAPTER XXI

THE TRAP

You remember such times as that, if ever any other man went through what I went through then. And I can remember the particular bush that was just before me. I never knew its name. I don't think I ever saw another one quite like it. The leaf was rather pale, and had a bright, varnished look, and the stems were covered with a white bark. I looked at all the waverings and the tremblings of those leaves in the wind, and remember them now so well that I could almost count them out, one by one. And all the time I was shuddering as I thought of the agony of the poor Chief.

"Look here, Chief," I said. "This fellow Loomis is out of his head about Sue Carr. And she's fond of me, Chief, and she'll keep Loomis from doing me any harm. She's mighty clever, and she'll manage pretty well to keep Loomis in hand. Don't you worry about me. Take care of yourself, and get away from here. Ferrald, he's likely to come sifting back through these woods, when he gets tired of waiting for you down in Culver Canyon."

"That girl loves you, Rickie," said the Chief, "and there's enough devil in Loomis for him to find it out, before long. And then—Heaven help you! And if I don't give myself up for you—"

His voice had been trembling, and now it broke completely. The thing I had been dreading happened. He began to sob in the frightful way that I could remember. And through the muffled sobbing I could hear the words working their way:

"Rickie, pray for me—pray to God that I can find the courage to do the right thing!"

Well, all at once I *wanted* to die. I would have been glad to die, to take this curse away from him. But what could I do, except to stammer at him, and beg him to go away, and to groan at him to stop worrying, because I would be all right in a short time.

Then the voice of Loomis yelled from the house: "Rickie, come back here. Turn around and walk straight back!"

I turned around and walked toward the house with the small, slow steps that the chains on my ankles permitted, and I heard my brother whisper:

"Rickie, forgive me! Forgive me!"

And I give you my word that everything went blank for me, and I couldn't see a thing except the imagined brutal face of the assistant warden who had broken the soul of my brother like a rotten stick.

"If you're not out of that brush and coming straight after him by the time he gets to the door of this house, Chief," yelled Loomis, "we'll blast him full of lead the minute he comes through the door!"

I think of it still—the ingenuity of Loomis in promising my brother the sight of me dead on the threshold of the room, so that every step I made would be right on the heartstrings of the Chief.

I could hear the Chief's broken voice as he began to

pray. He said: "Almighty God, give me strength! God, God, let me be a man!"

What I gave thanks for was that Loomis and the rest of his murderers inside of the house could not hear that broken voice.

"He's afraid to come!" shouted Loomis. "He's going to let the kid die for him! He's a rotten rat! Boys, get ready! We'll let the Chief see his kid brother blown full of holes. That'll do him some good. That'll be a thing for him to remember!"

I was close to that doorway, now, and I suppose that I slowed up a little. But, really, I think I was glad to be going in that direction, in any direction away from the horrible voice of the Chief. I went up to the doorway, and braced myself. It was hard to look into the dimness of that room and see the gleam of rifles leveled at me. I had to stick out my chest like a fool of a pouter pigeon, and pull in my chin, and grit my teeth, before I could lift my foot to the threshold. Then I heard a great voice that I hardly recognized as the voice of the Chief come ringing out from the trees behind me, calling: "Rickie, I'm coming! Loomis, you can have me!"

I looked back, and there was the Chief walking out from the trees, parting the last foliage of the bushes with his hands.

The agony he had been through had left his face white, but he walked in the old way that I knew, with his fine head raised high, and his step light on the ground, and that free-swinging stride that I've never seen the like of in any other man. He came smiling, I tell you!

And it sort of dropped into me like a rock into deep water that the dead soul of my brother had come to life again, and that somehow his prayer *had* been answered, and that this man who was walking toward the house to give himself for me was the one whom all those murdering rats inside the house had feared so much. He was born again; he was again the Chief!

Well, the two things hit me like two punches on each

side of the jaw. A darkness exploded across my brain. I hate to say what happened to me, but the fact is that I dropped in a dead faint half across the threshold, and half sprawling on the ground outside.

They were picking me up, when I came to. They were lifting me by the nape of the neck, like a dead dog. It was Little Charlie who had me that way, pulling me up to my feet. As I opened my eyes, I saw a thing that brought all of my wits back to me—it was the Chief, standing there with manacles on his arms and on his legs, and with his head as high as ever, and the color in his face, and a bright glory shining out of his eyes, as he smiled at those sneaking, glowering faces all around him.

It came on me again that this man was to be thrown away because of me, and that all he might be to the world was to be wiped out because he happened to have a dolt of a brother who blindly got into trouble. The weight of that grief and shame and regret nearly blotted me out again, so that Little Charlie shook me, and muttered savagely in my ear:

"Stand up! Stand up! Or somebody'll be thinking that you're afraid, or something like that!"

I would have wanted to laugh, at any other time, and even as it was, I grinned a little, perhaps, when I glanced up and aside at Little Charlie and at the bruised swollen, blue-battered eyes which he wore. He insisted on being proud of me as of a formidable, terrible man queller.

But my glance at Little Charlie was only a glance. My look, my whole soul went back to the Chief. As I saw how he dominated, even in chains, all of those outlaws who stood about the room, my grief increased. Very few of them had put down their rifles. They remained standing in an attitude of strained attention, ready for anything, and the grimness of preparation had not yet begun to give way to an air of exultation. They were still incredulous. They could not actually believe that they were in possession of the Chief.

"Chief," I said, "I know you'll forgive me for being

125

the bait to the trap, but Heaven will never forgive me. I wish that I'd never been born."

He started to say something gracious and kindly, and then the rapid, barking voice of Loomis broke in and drowned his words.

"You, Levin, and you, Thomason, get out with horses and start a patrol. Use your brains and use your eyes. There's got to be a surety that none of the friends of the Chief are hanging back, waiting for his signal before they close in."

"I have no men out there," said the Chief.

"You mean that you came up here alone?" demanded Loomis, gaping at him. It was an odd thing to see Loomis startled half out of his foxy wits.

"I came up here alone," said the Chief. "I'll never again lead other men into trouble. And even if I had a thousand men out there, I'd have Rickie tell them to scatter and go home, when he rode out of the valley. I'd like to send a few messages of another sort by him to some friends of mine, though. Last wishes. You can hear them, or read them, if you want to."

"Yeah, maybe I'll hear them," Loomis told him, "but Rickie's not going out. He's staying here with you!"

The Chief, in that moment when he had the realization that he had given up his life for nothing, that he had put himself into the trap without setting me free, made no sudden movement. He simply raised his head a trifle higher and turned his steady eye on Loomis.

"You've simply bought me with a lie. Is that the way of it, Loomis?" said he.

Loomis shrank a little, in front of that big, calm man. Even with the chains on his hands and feet, there was something mighty about the Chief, and something awe-inspiring. Harry Loomis actually gave back half a step before he realized that he was being shamed before all his men. Then he strode forward and shook his fist under the chin of my brother, and shouted:

"Yes, I've got you, I bought you with a trick, and a smart trick. I've got you and I've got your brother, too.

126

I've got the whole poisonous brood of you so that after you die, nobody'll think of lifting a hand because of you. I've got you the way I've always sworn I'd get you. And you're helpless—and I can do what I want with you!"

As he finished saying that he whipped the back of his hand across the face of the Chief, so that the skin was broken, and a little trickle of blood began to run slowly down toward his chin. But not a shadow of fear, not a spark of anger appeared in the eyes of the brother.

I felt the blow on my naked heart, and then instantly I was glorying that there could be such a man in the world.

"Loomis," he said, "you have me here, and you can, as you say, do exactly what you please with me. But I want to beg you to see that it's a different matter with my brother. He's only a youngster of twenty-two, Harry. He's never lifted his hand against any man until he came into the mountains, trying to do what he thought was my job. He's no great gun expert. He's not naturally a fighting man. If you let him go, I'll get his sworn oath that he'll never lift a hand against you. I'll make him swear to forget everything that he's seen and heard in this place.

"Besides, you've got to think of another thing. You have a lot of men here who are following you. And I've had men who followed me, too. Not one of them ever betrayed me, because every man of my crew knew that what I said was the truth, and that I'd stick to my word as if I were forged to it with steel. But here you're showing all of your men that your word isn't worth a twist of straw. They'll never trust you, after they've seen you break faith with me. It's bad policy for you to do this, Loomis."

I still think of that speech, and something works in the marrow of my spine when I remember the calm, persuasive, logical voice of the speaker. I recall, too, how those snakes who followed Loomis looked suddenly askance at one another, as though they were registering the truth of what they heard. I suppose that Loomis, too, must have been aware that his crowd was making comparisons between him and their captive.

However, he had a lucky point on which he would make his answer.

"You say he's just a kid, do you? He isn't *able* to do us any harm, eh? Why, that's a lie and a loud lie, and you know it! We know it, too. Who smashed Little Charlie, there, like a rotten apple? Who fought it out with Sammy Went, the slickest gun fighter that ever pulled a Colt out of a holster? Who had the nerve to come up here and almost fool the lot of us?

"Why, this same kid brother of yours has done all of those things, and now you try to make a pack of fools of us, don't you? But we're not half-wits! We've got brains enough to know what he is, and we've got brains enough to know that we've got to blot out the pair of you, or else we've only scotched the snake, and not killed it. We have you. The only thing we need to decide is how we're going to crucify you so that the whole world will know what happens to the enemies of the Loomis boys. Em and Sting Ray, take the pair of 'em up into the attic, and watch 'em like your own eyes. If you blink—they may both turn into smoke before you open your eyes again."

CHAPTER XXII

DEATH WATCH

IT was not, properly, like hobbling up the ladder into a room. It was more like going into a maw of death. The sun was working high in the sky, now, and the room was very hot. Looking out the window, I could see the thin mist rising like a breath from the face of the lake, and the noonday dimness covering everything, and pushing back the mountains to a greater distance. The Chief and I were made to sit with our backs against the wall, facing the window, because in that way there was always a steady light on us, and what the guards wanted.

The room itself was long and low with the cross-rafters not much more than five feet from the floor. Those rafters were just saplings that had been trimmed and put in place. The trimming had been done so roughly that here and there a small twig still projected, and to one of them clung a little brown leaf, curled into a knot.

You get to notice small things like that, when you're thinking of death. You can even count the beats of your heart and watch the throb of the artery in your wrist, and start wondering at the beauty of the machine that keeps us living.

Emory and Sting Ray had fetched up a pair of stools that they could sit on while they smoked cigarettes, or chewed, and spat oblong streaks across the floor.

Now and then they would get up and take a step or two on the sagging floor, and when they did that, somebody in the room beneath always yelled up and swore at them for knocking down so much dust. And they would yell back, just as loudly, and curse the job that kept them cooped up in a hot oven.

The Sting Ray went to the trapdoor once, and swore that the killing of us was the main job, and that it didn't matter how the thing was done. But somebody bawled up to him to be patient for a little while, because Loomis was getting hold of an idea that would make red Indians look like a bunch of pikers.

In the meantime, the Chief and I talked together, in low voices so that Sting Ray and Em could not hear much of what we said. And all the while, like a death drone, I could make out the murmurings of the men downstairs who were planning the best ways to kill us. Sometimes their voices went up into a bawling laughter as one of them got hold of an idea specially brutal, and specially grotesque.

In the first place, I told the Chief exactly what had happened to me. I made the account short, but I put in all of the essential details. When I got to Sue Carr, I paused a little, and I told him that she was active as a bird, and that she was sure to find out, before long, that we were prisoners, and then she might bring us some kind of help.

The Chief looked at me with his quiet eye. There was pity in it, but there was a lot of grave decision, too, as though he couldn't endure me to keep on nursing foolish illusions.

"You have to remember that the distances are pretty long, up here in the mountains, Rickie," he said gently.

And I felt like a fool—I and my silly hopes! Except that it kept seeming to me that we couldn't die. Not together. There was too much strength and importance to the Chief. I didn't matter. But somehow, he couldn't die in a wretched, helpless way, like this. It couldn't be in the cards.

That was the hope and the feeling that I kept on matching against the muttering sounds of those voices down below.

But still the truth of what the Chief had said kept coming back to me—that the distances in these mountains were pretty long—and I realized that even after Sue discovered we were held captive, she would need the wings of a bird to get together a crowd of men strong enough to help us. I doubted, for instance, if she could raise a group in Blue Water. Too many of the people there made indirect or direct profits out of the operations of the robbers. And they probably would be afraid to move as a posse unless they were two or three score strong. At the best, it would take a full day to get to Blue Water and back again with them. And that was far too long to do us the slightest good.

I learned from the Chief what had happened to him, and I wish that I could remember, so as to put everything down in his own words, because they would be a lot better than mine.

He said that after he left the house, the day had been pretty bad for him, and he kept on wondering what my plan had been. At last, that evening, he came back and found that mother was sitting out on the front veranda, where she'd fallen asleep with the moon shining in her face, and her tired head fallen over on her shoulder; and the cold of the night kept her trembling in her sleep.

The Chief said that as he looked at her, he felt a great pity and love, such as he'd never felt before. He wanted to put out his hands and take hold of her, and comfort not her body only but her whole soul. And he said that he realized how often he had looked at her with a touch of contempt, or of displeasure, at the least, because she had seemed to him rather a low cut, from time to time. But from that moment forward, he would know the proper way to value her.

He waked her up, and he said that it was a strange thing to see the sleep and the surprise go out of her face, and the love come into it. He got her back into the house, asking where I was. She said that I had gone off deer hunting. I had left a note for him in his room.

He got that note and read it, and made out that something strange was in the air. When he stepped out into the hallway again, Mother was waiting for him.

She went up to him and asked: "Is there trouble for Rickie, my dear?"

"Yes," he said. "There's trouble."

"I knew it," said my mother. "He was born for grief, like me. Is it just this man Ferrald, or is it on account of you?"

"It's on account of me, mostly," the Chief told her.

For he said that when he looked down into the pain in her face, his talent for lying melted away out of him and left him as weak as air. He had to tell her every truth.

But after she found out that the trouble for me was coming through the Chief, she didn't urge him to do anything about it. She simply said:

"He loves you, my dear son." And she left it at that, and said good night to him.

After that, he was in a terrible quandry, the Chief said. He wanted to do something about me. He guessed that I had gone off on the trail with Ferrald. He almost knew that that was what I had done. And he wanted to follow, because he could guess that our trail would point toward Loomis, and he knew that Loomis could be found in the Blue Waters. But like a horse under the spur and a strong pull on the reins, all he could do was to tremble. His heart leaped in him, but could not make him decide. And the prison shakes came over him.

They left him as weak as a child. He knew that he wouldn't be able to ride on the trail. If he did ride on it, there would be no strength in him to fight when the pinch came, even supposing that he caught up with Ferrald and me in time.

He decided, after all, that he had better take my first advice and simply leave the country, because he could be worth nothing while he was in it. So he went out and caught up a horse, saddled it, and rode over to the house of Jerome Benchley. He knocked at the door, till somebody wakened inside. It was Jerry Benchley himself who came down and opened the door and stood back in his night shirt and trousers, with a lamp in one hand and a gun in the other.

The Chief said, simply, that he was going on a long trip and starting at once, and he wanted to know if he could say good-by to Allardyce.

"Are you leaving us for good?" asked old Benchley. And the Chief answered: "Yes, I think I am."

Benchley looked at him for a minute and then said: "Well, it's the business of Allardyce to condemn you. Not mine. Men and women, men and women, they're what keep trouble floating in the world!"

He went away, and pretty soon Allardyce came hurrying down, alone, holding a wrap around her shoulders, and her hair shining down her back, so that she looked, with the fear in her eyes, like a child.

She ran up to the Chief and asked him if it was true, and if he was really leaving her forever. And right then and there, as he started to tell her the truth, the prison shakes came back on him and shook the manhood out of his heart, and made him into the thing that I had seen back there in our dining room the night before.

I asked the Chief how she endured it, and he told

me that she simply sat close to him, and waited, and kept one hand always stroking his head, while he groaned out the true story of what had happened to him, just as he had told it to me. He told her everything else—and how he was afraid that I had gone up into the mountains to find Loomis, with Ferrald.

She waited a while longer, and then she said that he would have to go, too. He told her that it was no good, that she had seen how even talking to her had broken him down, and that the sight or even the thought of a fight would wreck him again.

Well, what do you think she said to him them?

She looked him bang in the eye and said: "It's better to die quickly, Chief, than to keep living in fear of yourself. You may not be able to die well, but at least you can die in your own boots instead of in your brother's."

He was so amazed when she said this, that it shocked half the shuddering out of him.

She went on to say that it had been a horrible shock that had taken the temper out of the steel in him, and that if he thrust himself into the fire again, perhaps the temper would be brought back to him once more.

What gave a girl like that such wisdom? I can't tell. But something made her guess. And out there in front of the old cabin, as he watched me walk back toward the door, the fire got hold of my brother and burned him clean, and turned him from brittle metal into the true steel again.

He said, and I know he meant it, that he had sorrow enough for me, and sorrow for Allardyce, too; but for himself, he was simply happy, because it was better to live one instant as he used to be and then face any sort of a death of torture, than it was to exist in the hell that he had been wandering in since that terrible day in the prison when the manhood all ran out of his soul.

The Chief had finished this story of his, when we heard a noise outside of the house, and a lot of chattering voices, suddenly. And after a while, up comes the face of the great Loomis through the trapdoor, and he stood there before us, with the smile always beginning on his mouth, and always twisting it a little to the side.

"Chief," he said, "the pair of you have a respite. Because a fellow's coming who hates your heart almost as much as I do. Lefty Payson's coming to join up forces with me. Understand? He's coming to throw in with me and be *second* to me. Get that? And I'm going to save the bonfire until he arrives. He hates you, and he has reason to hate you; and I wouldn't cheat a good friend like Lefty out of his chance to see the finish of you! Besides, he may have some ideas to use on you in the final scene. You know he's a man with imagination."

And he stood there and laughed at us, silently, like a gray wolf.

CHAPTER XXIII

CARR'S RESOLVE

BEFORE the finish of the strangest day that any man ever lived through, I have to tell you about one more thing.

It started that afternoon when Susan Carr rode her little black mare through the canyon, and sent it galloping toward the lake, and the cabin of Loomis. She came through a grove of trees, going lickety-split, when a rider pulled out of the next wood and waved an arm at her.

She pulled up, and saw that it was Thomason, a long-faced fellow who came up grinning, and still waving his hand.

"I dunno that you'd better go on to the house," he said.

"Why not?" asked Sue.

"Because," answered Thomason, "there's going to be high jinks over there before long, and when they happen, maybe Loomis won't want you around."

"What sort of jinks?" she asked.

"High ones," said Thomason. "There's a thing gone

134

and happened today that folks ain't never going to forget. The Chief came in and gave himself up to keep his brother from getting shot. And now Loomis is foxy enough to keep 'em both, and they're both going to be turned off together, as soon as Loomis thinks up the best way of doing the job."

She sat her horse and looked down at the ground for a moment.

"Well," she said to Thomason, "I'll go and see if Harry wants me to stay off the place."

"All right," said Thomason. "I ain't fool enough to say no to you."

She rode straight on until the trees of the next grove covered her. Then she cut across to a gully, and raced the mare down it, and so finally made a half circle and cut back onto the trail that led toward her house. The sun was dropping all the while toward the west, and every foot that it seemed to slide brought death that step closer to the Chief and to me, she thought.

Well, when she reached the house, there was her father with all his rifles laid out in the sun. He'd been cleaning them and getting them ready ever since she had told him about my being a prisoner in the hands of Loomis. Neither of them knew what to do. They both thought, of course, that it would be useless to try to come close to the house of Loomis with a large body of men, because at the sound of the approach, Loomis would be sure to murder me before he ran for it with his gang.

Sue Carr made straight for her father, and threw herself off her horse, and told him the story as she had it from Thomason. She looked west toward the sun. It was too late, she said, even to bring a hope of any rescue, because Loomis would be certain to kill the Chief before it was dark.

Big Ralph Carr took a look at her and then he took a look at the sun. After that, he ran to the corral, caught up the one horse that was really strong enough to carry his weight, saddled it, took a rifle, a pair of revolvers, plenty of ammunition, and rode off the place.

He did all of this without speaking a word, though Sue kept begging him to speak to her.

Finally, as she cantered the mare beside him, he said briefly:

"I've lived like a pig in a sty letting the other swine root around me. If Rickie is dead, it's my fault. I never should have let him drift into the hands of Loomis. Now I'm going to pay the penalty."

"It's too late!" she cried at him. "And what can you do, alone?"

"Go back to the house!" he commanded, and would not speak again.

She kept trying to argue until she saw that his mind was as set as stone. She could see the finish of me already accomplished—because the sun was almost down; and now she saw her father throwing himself into the same whirlpool. The world was ending for Sue, as she followed that giant of a man through the mountains, and somehow he seemed to have forgotten that she was anywhere near him.

It was the red of the sunset when they came over the first divide, above the trees, and found a tall fellow in the trail just before them, tightening up the cinches of his saddle, which was on a tired run of a mustang. That tall man was Ferrald.

Jim had been down in Culver Canyon as usual to wait for some sign of the Chief, and this time his patience was pretty well burned up. He was so mad at the Chief for leaving him in the lurch, and so full of his own bitter thoughts, that he had not heard the squeaking of saddle leather as the two of them came up the trail. Now he moved to get out of the way, but he realized that he had been seen. The presence of the girl made him feel that it was all right, and presently he recognized the bulk of Ralph Carr.

When Carr came up to him, he reached out his hand and put it on Ferrald's shoulder.

136

"Stranger, which way are you heading?" he asked.

"Yonder," said Ferrald, waving a hand at half the sky.

"Could you use a job?" asked Carr.

"What sort of a job?" asked Ferrald.

"A fighting job," said Carr.

"That depends on who the fight's with," answered Jim Ferrald.

"Beyond those hills," said Ralph Carr, "there's a pack of coyotes running behind a leader called Harry Loomis. Tell me, did you ever hear of him?"

This sounded all right to Ferrald, I suppose.

"I've heard of Loomis, and his tricks; I've heard of his teeth, too," he replied.

"If you're afraid of them, there's no use talking to you," said Carr. "But for a fighting man, tonight, I'd give a thousand dollars, if I have to mortgage my soul to raise the coin."

At that, Ferrald came closer, and squinted up at Carr.

"If you're not talkin' through your hat," he said, "I might ride along with you just for luck, and not for money. What's up?"

"A friend of mine is having his throat cut by that gang, about this time of day, I suppose," said Carr. "His name you wouldn't know. He's Rickie Willard, the brother of the man they call the Chief."

"Not know him?" shouted Ferrald. "Is Loomis after him? Does Loomis know his real name?"

"He does," said Carr, "and Loomis has the Chief in his hands, too."

That blasted the ground away from under Ferrald.

He got the story after he had jumped into the saddle. He agreed with Carr that the pair of them might be able to make some sort of a surprise attack, if they pushed on, because if Loomis had killed me and the Chief, he and his gang would be celebrating and not worrying about anything under the sun.

As for Carr, he had made up his mind to clean his record with fire. And as for Ferrald, I always felt that he would be willing to take a mortal wound for the sake of fighting it out with Loomis.

Anyway, they only halted to tell Sue that she would have to go back home.

She said good-by, turned back down the trail, and then swung about and followed on. The idea of going back to the dark of that house in the hollow, and of waiting there for news of what had happened to everybody that was dear to her in the world was too much for her. Besides, she was the sort of a person who would want to be in at the death, no matter what amount of danger was in the air.

So she trailed the pair of them through the mountains, as the night settled down, and the stars came out. Finally down they worked into the hollow valley where the house of Loomis stood, and from the distance they saw the shining of the lights.

CHAPTER XXIV

LEFTY PAYSON

I'VE had to go back and pick up a lot of threads to make you understand what was drawing to a focus around the house of Loomis, there in the shallow valley where he and his thugs hung out. Now I want to get straightforward with what happened inside of the house.

That afternoon went on pretty slowly, for the Chief and me. You'd say that two men who had not long to live would find time dragging, but as a matter of fact the watching of that pot made it seem to boil all the slower.

Not even the Sting Ray could speed things up. Em grew bored with guarding us, and sat against the wall and took a nap, now and then, but Sting liked his work. He had been so broken and bruised physically that there was nothing worth while for him in the world except watching pain that other people had to suffer, as well as himself. Now and then he would run his yellow-stained eyes over us, and smile a little, and take out his keys and spin them on their string, around and around his forefinger.

He said nothing. He didn't need to say anything, except to show us the keys that fitted our irons, and smile. I wondered at the look in his handsome, marred face as he sat there and tormented us, silently. At least, it was a torment to me, but the Chief seemed perfectly calm and undisturbed.

Em started one bit of conversation with the Chief. "Why does Lefty Payson hate you so much?" Em asked.

The Chief considered Em for a moment, that weak face with the savage, leering eyes, and then he decided to answer. He said: "Why, it's an old story, Emory."

"Yeah," said Emory, sneering, "most of your stories would be about three years old, anyway."

The Chief waited a moment, then he went on: "Lefty joined up with my boys, one time. But while we were riding across the country, he did a little raiding of his own. He came across a boy riding a mustang that appealed to Lefty's eye. So he kicked the boy off and took the horse for himself. I happened to be in eyeshot of that, so I gave the horse back to the boy."

"Just like that? And Lefty didn't make a kick?" asked Em.

"Lefty kicked as hard as he could," said the Chief. "After I got through with him, however, he decided that he'd leave the boy alone. I took his guns away from him, and his horse, too, and let him hoof it out of the mountains. After that, he had quite a grudge against me. He'll be glad to join the party to-night."

"And I don't blame him," said Emory. "If you done that to me, I'd cut your heart out. Know that?"

The Chief smiled at him. His smile made Emory flush to the hair. He leaped up and began to shout. But the Chief just went on smiling and after a while Emory sat down again, and seemed a little ashamed of himself for abusing a man in chains who couldn't hit back.

I looked Em over carefully. Take him all in all, he

was about the most worthless cur that I ever saw wearing the boots of a man. There was only one thing to say about him, that his teeth were as sharp as they were yellow.

But that story of Lefty Payson gave me the chills, all right. The sort of malice that was in Lefty would not be any weaker just because three or four years had gone by since the time of his humiliation. No, he could be depended on to nurse his poison and keep it fresh.

After a while, when the sun went down, Em went down the ladder and made a tremendous fuss because he said that it was unfair to keep him up there in that pigpen, watching the prisoners. But Loomis sent him back, saying:

"The longer you stay up there, the more you'll hate that pair of brothers for keeping you there, and the more you hate that pair of brothers, the closer you'll keep your eyes on 'em. Go back there and remember what I told you before—that if you so much as blink an eye, the two of 'em are likely to go up in smoke and disappear! Now get back there and stay on the job, and dont' let me see your face down here again!"

Emory came back and sat and snarled to himself, and gritted his teeth, and twisted up his weak, cruel face with rage and hate.

"Sometime I'll get him!" he said, more to himself than to us.

"No," said the Chief to my surprise, "a cruel little cur like you will never have the nerve to tackle a fellow like Loomis."

Those words raised Emory to his feet as though a strong hand had taken him by the nape of the neck and lifted him. He got up and gasped and started to run at my brother, but Sting Ray stopped him with a word.

"You're nutty," he said.

Emory stopped short. He was gasping and panting with fury.

"You can't have this dish all to yourself. You poor

140

fool, ain't you able to see that he wants to get you mad enough to shoot him through the head? He ain't hankering after what's going to happen to him when Lefty gets here!"

"No matter what the rest of 'em think up," said Emory, "I'm going to have an extra special twist to give things. I know what *I'm* going to do!"

Whatever the idea was that came to him, he groaned with the joy of it. He fairly writhed, as he stared at the Chief and thought of the happy time that was coming.

A little after this, the Chief lay down on his side, pillowed his head on his arm, and pretended to be sleeping. But I knew, somehow, that sleep was a thousand miles from him. He had thought of some device; something had come into that fertile brain of his.

From that minute, I was in a whirl of excitement. Perhaps it was some simple contrivance that was in his mind; perhaps it was some desperately complicated thing. In any case, he would not risk speaking to me about it, for fear that one word overheard would be enough to give us away. He just lay there with his legs drawn up close to his body, and made his breathing regular and deep and long, and all the while he was smoothing the lines out of his face, and making it placid as stone. But the more placid it became, the more certain I was that he was awake.

There was no proof of it, however—just an occasional swift flutter of the eyelashes.

It was long after darkness when Lefty Payson arrived. He came up the ladder shortly afterwards and leaned over and peered at the Chief asleep. Lefty was the gorilla type. When he smiled, it seemed to be only with his upper lip, not with the lower one. He just leaned over and looked at the Chief, and smiled, and he made me think of a cook who goes out into the poultry yard and picks out with his eyes the nice fat rooster that he's going to cook, pretty soon.

Lefty Payson said nothing at all, but just went down the ladder again. Then Emory thought of something that he wanted to say and hurried halfway down the ladder after Lefty, calling out to him, and Lefty answering. Downstairs there was a good deal of confusion, just now. Everybody was excited by the arrival of Lefty, since it meant two important things—first, that he really was going to throw his brutality and experience behind Loomis, and second, that the time had come to dispose of the Chief and me. I suppose they were all milling over their last fine ideas of how to dispose of the Chief, when, as he lay there on the floor of the attic room, he acted.

Then Sting Ray, after following Lefty to the top of the ladder, and watching him and Em go down, turned away and came back across the room, and gave a wicked smile down at the Chief as he went by. That instant the two legs of the Chief shot out like a catapult and knocked Mr. Sting Ray's feet cleanly out from under him.

There wasn't time for Sting to turn, or even to gasp, or to yell, but down he came with a crash straight on top of me.

Well, I wasn't sitting there idle, either. The moment that the Chief kicked Sting into the air, the moment I saw the line of his fall, I knew that action was needed, and I was ready for some share of it. I got my wrists together, and as Sting Ray dropped, I banged him across the head with my handcuffs.

"What the devil is that up there?" shouted the voice of Loomis, below.

We were silent. We had to be silent, though the Chief already had the keys to the irons out of the pocket of Sting Ray.

Sting lay on his back, still as a mouse, dead to the world, with a trickle of blood running down from a cut on his scalp, while the Chief fitted the keys into my handcuffs, and then into my leg irons, and with two twists made me a free man.

That was what he would do—give me the first fighting chance for my life!

I had one of the guns of Sting Ray, by this time. I

142

shoved the other toward the Chief, and taking the keys, unlocked his irons. He was free, too, as we heard Loomis yell, below:

"Get back there where you belong, will you, Emory?"

"Aw, what could happen?" said Emory, and the ladder began to creak as he came back up it.

Well, I was ready to go for that trapdoor, but the Chief was moving before me, and he was getting across that floor without making a noise!

No, he wasn't exactly moving across the floor. Rather, he was skirting around it. No human being could have moved silently across that rotten old batch of boards, not even with the spirits to help them along and lighten them up. But the Chief was skirting around the edges of the floor, right close to the wall, where of course there was less leverage.

Anyway, there he went stealing, and gave me one bright, terrible glance out of his eyes that told me he was enjoying this moment. I could remember then what I had heard before—that he was different from other men because he loved battle. He loved it for its own sake, and not for any reward that he might get out of it.

And just as Emory came up the ladder, lifting his head and shoulders above the level of the attic floor, the Chief struck him with both hands, the way an eagle strikes a smaller bird.

I mean, the instant he put his hands on Em, he seemed to knock all consciousness out of the man, just the way an eagle will knock the life out of a duck, say, if it strikes its talons into it in swooping.

And there was the Chief dragging Emory right up through the trapdoor, and the body of Em hanging down loose and limp, and his head falling over on one shoulder, while a terrible yell went up from the gang below.

Somehow, they all seemed to have seen the thing at the same glance. I could make out of that general roar the frightened screech of Loomis himself, and then the tremendous note of Little Charlie thundering out above the rest.

"It means that Sting Ray's gone crazy—or crazy crooked!" bellowed Charlie. "He's joined up with the pair of 'em. He's turned 'em loose! The Chief is loose!"

I heard that voice bellowing, as I caught one of the guns of Emory that the Chief threw to me, while he pocketed the other.

He turned away from the trapdoor. Because it was clear that nobody would be fool enough, at any rate, to attempt to swarm up that ladder when armed men were at the head of it.

"Burn the house down with the pair of 'em in the attic. There's no way they can get out!" shouted some one.

And while they were yelling the Chief had picked up the body of Emory by the heels. He turned himself twice around, like a hammer thrower heaving out the weight, and then slammed the full weight of that body, face forward, into the boards that made the wall of the attic on the south side. Those boards were not well fastened in. And the weight of that terrible blow smashed them open, and the body of Emory crashed through the gap that was made.

It was big enough for both of us to squeeze through in turn, after the Chief had torn off another board with his bare hands. Then we lay out there on the slanting roof that extended back from this upper part of the building, because only a part of the house was built two stories.

I saw life and freedom there before me in a wide swing of the eye around the mountains, and under the stars; and the whole taste of this good existence was in my heart, I can tell you. I felt that I should be able to fight like a giant.

Well, most of the fight went out of me in the next two seconds.

First, the body of Emory, which the Chief, of course, had let go of, rolled side over side down the slope of the roof, and before either of us could catch the senseless man, he had fallen down, out of sight.

Next, right on the heels of that, a ball of fire shot up through the air and landed on the roof beside us, and showed us up as well as any torch could have done.

What had happened?

Well, it seemed to me that the sky was raining fire on our unlucky heads, but it simply meant that somebody— Loomis, I suppose—had been able to think ahead of us, like lightning, and had dipped some waste in kerosene out of one of the lamps, and lighting it, he had chucked it up there on the roof to illuminate a target.

It was a beautiful light, all right, and down there in the darkness, secure among the shadows, there were some excellent shots to take advantage of that good break.

Something slashed my cheek, and made the cut which still stings me extra deep when a cold wind works down to the roots of the scar tissue. And other bullets winged by me like wasps.

I wouldn't have had the sense to do anything except to try to crawl back through the hole out of which we had come, but the Chief did better than that. He knocked the burning ball of waste off the roof with a bullet from his gun, and as it dropped down into the blackness, it threw out a wide pool of light that showed several of the figures of the gunmen.

Other balls of fire would follow, and that roof was bound to be a mighty unhealthy place for us, but for the instant, we were in darkness, and the other fellows were lighted. I used that instant to slide back through the hole in the wall into the attic, where I saw Sting Ray gradually sitting up, his head sagged down on his breast.

The Chief, however, couldn't run until he had put one shot into those devils. I heard his gun bark a second time, and a wild screech of pain followed it—a screech that was cut off short, as though a hand had been clapped suddenly over the poor fellow's mouth.

It was the hand of death, I could guess easily enough.

145

CHAPTER XXV

BLUE FLAMES

By the time the Chief was back inside the attic room, more balls of fire were landing on the roofs, and more bullets were whipping through the gap in the wall which the Chief had battered open with that human club. We ducked over as we went for the trapdoor, driving Sting Ray ahead of us. We took him between us, as we went down the ladder.

It was walking out of a high hell into a lower one. That was all. The bullets made the hell in the second-story attic; and fire made the hell down below.

They had simply taken a can of kerosene, to judge by the smell and the blue of the flames, and scattered the oil at random, and dropped a match. I had heard the puff of the slight explosion when the flame ran wild.

Now the stifling black fumes were filling the air, and the floor was trailed across by welters of the blue flame, but chiefly along the walls they had spilled the oil, and there the fire was catching everywhere. There was no use thinking of putting that fire out. Every room in that house was catching. They must have run through the whole place scattering the oil, giving a five-gallon can of it a swing as they went through each chamber, and now the heat was rising.

The wood was catching rapidly, too. For the sun had dried out and seasoned that unpainted wood for just such a moment as this, and it was catching like tinder.

We stumbled through the fumes. I was trying to think, but fear and the choking breath of the fire were a lot too much for me. All I could do was to see the figure of the Chief leading the way, and to make out that Sting Ray followed him.

When we came into the last room, the kitchen, there was no fire at all inside, but a big blaze was shooting up outside the door. The reason was plain, because the fellow who distributed the oil—that same devil of a Loomis, no doubt—had jumped through the kitchen door, slammed it shut behind him, and then flung the rest of the oil over the outer wall of the house. In a solid blue sheet the flames rose past the window of the kitchen, and gave us a sort of grisly light for seeing one another.

The three of us stood there and looked at one another. The Chief came up and gave a glance to the wound that was pouring blood down my face and over my clothes, but he said nothing about tying it up. It was too apparent that we had come to our last minutes of life, and the extra drain of a little blood made hardly any difference to us just then.

But now, as we stood there listening to the roar of the oil flames, and to the crackling noises as the wood was ignited in all parts of the house, I want to call attention to some of the words and the actions of the Sting Ray, because they're worth remembering.

When we first came into the kitchen, he stopped in the middle of the floor and said above the noise of the fire:

"Well, boys, here's the sample package of the place we're traveling to. I might 'a' know that the fire would burn blue for us!"

When he had said this, he laughed a little.

After that, he went over to the stove, where there was a big iron pot full of beans, stewing. They were all red with Mexican peppers and tomatoes. Sting got hold of a big iron spoon and stirred up that mess and then tasted a few of the beans.

"Little Charlie is a fool in most ways," said Sting Ray, "but he's a cook, I'm telling you!"

He turned around, with the big spoon heaped with beans and offered it to us. I actually shook my head at the beans, and then Sting deliberately gestured with the heaped spoon toward the Chief, saying:

"No use cheating your stomach, even if you're only ten minutes from hell, boys!"

So he put the spoon into his mouth and brought it out

cleaned of the beans. He smacked his lips over the big mouthful, and shook his head to indicate how good those beans were.

I never saw such a man. I never saw a man who seemed to me, just then, to have such possibilities in the world, where he would never have a chance to use them.

The Chief said to him: "Sting, if you can make your friends outside hear you, you're welcome to get out. I'll take no pleasure in seeing you burn to a crisp alongside of us. Neither will Rickie. Go on and try your luck."

Then Sting Ray stared agape, his mouth still full of the beans. He was able to understand death and even the hell he had been talking about, filled with the blue of fire, but he wasn't able to understand such a suggestion as the Chief had made to him, just now. He made one or two futile gestures, to illustrate words that he could not speak. Finally, he half choked himself, like a bird swallowing too big a morsel, and after he had rid his throat of the beans, he gasped out:

"You mean you want me to step out—and help the rest of 'em shoot you down when you're burned out of your place?"

"All right," said the Chief. "One more gun turned on us won't make a very great difference."

At this, Sting Ray walked straight up to the Chief and looked him full in the eye for a long moment, until the Chief was no longer smiling. Very seriously, they stared at one another, and what went on in their minds I could guess at only dimly.

Suddenly Sting burst out: "I'm staying right here with you, Chief. I ain't got long ahead of me, anyway, and I'd rather sort of have clean hands today, dying with the fool pair of you, than to save my rotten hide by walking out the door and siding with those stinking rats out yonder."

I listened to that speech with more wonder than I had ever listened to any words that I had heard before in my entire life. Take it all in all, I think that the performance of Sting Ray, from the moment he came down

148

into that kitchen, stood entirely by itself, and apart from anything that anybody else has ever seen in this world.

The Chief was moved. He put his left hand on the shoulder of Sting, and took the right hand of Sting Ray in his own. They didn't pump up and down. They just gripped each other, and looked, and looked, as though each of them were seeing a real man for the first time. I thought that they'd keep on standing there until the house burned down with a crash right over our heads.

They came out of the trance presently. The Chief quickly pulled a gun out and said: "Here, take this, Sting."

"Thanks," said Sting Ray. "If you don't mind, I'd rather die giving them a charge than waiting till we're cooked on one side and done brown on the other. Why not let the fire take this back door off its hinges and then charge out and get at them?"

The Chief turned to me, and I saw the gleaming of his eyes through the fumes and the smoke that filled the room. For the fire was gaining every minute, now. It was eating its way through the flimsy walls. It was gnawing at joists and beams. It was rubbing the boards thin and peering in at us with red eyes, here and there. Before long, the whole place might go smash.

You know that there's a crazy excitement about a fire. When you look at it, you get small impulses to go and throw yourself into the flames. Well, some of that excitement was rising in me—rising and roaring in me, as you might say. I trembled the way the flames trembled. I wanted to smash down that kitchen door and rush out at the devils who were waiting out yonder, secure, whooping and yelling, and pausing for the time when we'd be forced to run out of the house and let ourselves be shot down, one after the other.

The only thing I said was: "Well, I'm with you, Sting. Let's make a solid rush of it, shooting all the way."

"There are fellows out there," said the Chief, "who could pick off all three of us with three shots. There's no use being in a hurry. When we die, we'll be quite a time dead. And in the meantime, it's not so bad standing here and chatting."

"You're right," said Sting Ray, "except that the nearer the house comes to burning down, the closer they'll be watching to see us bolt out of the place. But there's a question I want to ask you. They say that you knew Bob Mulford. Is that right?"

"Yes," said the Chief.

"Did you know his girl?"

"The one with the red hair?"

"Yes, that's the one."

"I knew her," said the Chief.

"How did she look to you?" asked Sting Ray.

"One of the prettiest girls I ever saw," said the Chief.

"Good!" said Sting Ray, with a sigh as though he were very relieved. "I always thought so myself, but I wanted to get a good clear opinion from somebody who ought to know, before I go. You see, she used to be my girl, before she took up with Mulford."

Just then there was a frightful crashing as the roof came down through the attic floor and roared into the big bunk room. A gust of sparks, and a billow of flames and of smoke came shooting through the doorway into the kitchen.

"Now for it!" yelled Sting Ray.

The Chief grabbed him as he started for the rear door.

"Listen!" shouted the Chief.

The roaring of the flames that had shot up after the fall of the section of the roof died out a little, and even my duller ears could hear, from far away, the crackling of rifles, shooting fast, and the frightened yelling of men just outside the house.

The meaning of it came over me with a rush, of course. Men were taking the thugs of Loomis from the rear, and grinding them small, I hoped!

Then the Chief shouted out in a great voice: "We've got friends outside. We're going out, but not in a cluster. Sting, you take this rear door. I'll take the front one. Rickie, go out the side way. We'll make smaller targets.

Don't try to run, right away. Dive for the dark of the ground, and then creep forward away from the light of the house, if you can. Good-by, Sting!"

He took the hand of Sting Ray again. Then he turned and caught me in his arms, and I caught him, just the way he used to grab me when I was a small kid. Then he went off, and I stumbled ahead, somehow, and saw the Chief leaping through the dance of flames in the bunk room, making for the open front door. I had the easier job of knocking the side door open and going outside with a running jump.

When I landed, I dodged, and sprinted forward a few steps, still dodging and then dived for the ground, in a regular spread-eagle.

The wind was pretty well knocked out of me, but my eyes and ears were open, well enough.

I saw figures running to either side, among the trees, and through the brush. They were the men of Loomis! I recognized Little Charlie breaking for the corral, and catching a horse, and riding it wildly away, barebacked. They were all running for their lives, and off to each side I heard rifles firing rapidly, and great voices that shouted:

"Close in! Close in!"

It seemed to me that a whole regiment was gathering those rascals into a net.

CHAPTER XXVI

GUNMEN'S END

I SAW young Dill, his red hair blown straight back on his head, catch another horse and gallop it away. But the horse refused to run straight. It swerved off to the left, and I saw a monstrous shadow of a man rise up from the fire-lighted brush, and fire a rifle.

Dill tossed up his arms. His body streamed back off the horse, and it galloped away, riderless.

I got up, wild with excitement, and ran toward the brush, still dodging, but with a revolver ready in each hand. And then I saw, in another section of the bushes, two more figures leap up like two wild beasts, and close with one another. By the build of one of them, I knew that it was Ferrald.

I sprinted as hard as I could to come up in time to help him. The rest of the roof fell in, while I was on the way, and gave a magnificent light for me. But when I reached the spot, I was too late. Ferrald was done for, and the man who had mortally wounded him was trying to drag himself to his feet, but fell at once. That was Harry Loomis, himself.

Then I heard the thundering voice of Ralph Carr on my right, shouting:

"They're all here, as sound as new pennies. But what are *you* doing on this side of the fence, Sting Ray?"

"I changed horses in the middle of the stream," said Sting, panting, but as dry as you please.

And then there was a voice running straight toward me, a voice that rose into my mind like a fountain of bright water in the dark of a night.

That was Susan Carr. I barely got my arms around her, when she saw my face, and after that I was helpless until she had me bandaged.

Just what had been accomplished, I had no idea, at the time, except that I was pretty sure that Loomis's outfit had been pretty well smashed. As a matter of fact, as most of you know from the papers and the articles that were written at the time, Little Charlie and Sting Ray were the only ones of the lot who got away—they and poor Emory, whose face was so smashed that to carry it around with him the rest of his days will be punishment enough. As for Sting Ray, he got a free pardon on account of the way he had turned to our side in the middle of the fight. And I challenge anybody to say that that pardon was not deserved.

But to get back to what I actually saw before my eyes, by the light of the burning house of Loomis.

Carr had picked up Ferrald, but the body of poor Jim seemed to slide out of his hands, loosely.

"Set me down against that tree," said Jim Ferrald. "I wanta have a smoke. Has anybody got a cigarette he can roll for me? I'm dead for a smoke."

The Chief let Carr take charge of Ferrald, and he paid attention to Loomis.

Loomis had shot Ferrald three or four times through the body—I don't remember which number. I know that we tied a saddle blanket around him to stop the sight of the blood more than the flow of it. And Ferrald, who had used up his ammunition, had driven his knife into Loomis, again and again. Knife wounds are terribly painful, and Loomis was in agony.

However, he made a good finish. Strange to say, he wanted to be placed with his back against a tree, like Ferrald. They had mortally wounded each other and now they faced each other, and both of them were smoking cigarettes. Ferrald was calm as a cucumber, but Loomis was clear out of his head.

Sometimes he seemed to think that he was in the middle of the fight, again. Sometimes he was cursing and groaning because of his agony. Only once, just before the end, he recognized Sue Carr, and threw out his arms to her.

She surprised me by running right forward and dropping on her knees beside him. He seemed to think that she loved him. He still seemed to cling to that idea, and he grabbed her with both his arms, and told her that leaving her was all that made death a hard thing to him. He asked her to kiss him, and she did that, too. I made a move to go for her, but the Chief grabbed my shoulder and held me back.

Loomis said, before the finish: "God wouldn't let me have you. But just hoping to have you was happiness enough for me. Like the poor beggar, Sue, that got nothing but the fragrance of the roasting meat."

He actually tried to laugh, and then doubled right up in a screaming fit.

Sue stuck with him to the end. In his last agony, he sunk his teeth into one of his hands, and held on like a bulldog. Then, with a final twist of his legs, he turned on his face and lay still. Life certainly had a hard job tearing its way out of the body of that poor devil. I was in a cold sweat, watching him and listening to him.

Then I picked up Sue, and she was nearly dead herself. But right to the horrible finish, she wouldn't leave him. It made him happier to have her there, and she stuck by him. That's the sort of a person she is—never to let go, and as much mercy in her as there is courage.

Now, Ferrald had not opened his mouth, after getting the cigarette, but had sat there watching and listening to the dying of Loomis, and every time Loomis yelled, Ferrald nodded and grinned a little.

It was music to him, and that was plain.

"Squealed like a stuck pig, didn't he?" said Ferrald finally, looking at the dead body. "He got his, and he had a chance to know about it."

Big Ralph Carr was on his knee beside Ferrald, saying: "You fought them like a hero, man. But if only you hadn't rushed at that one, I would have rolled him over for you. I had a good bead on him, just as you ran in between!"

"And what good would it be if you'd killed him?" asked Ferrald. "What would there be to make my brother Jerry laugh, wherever he is, looking on? He'd have a fine opinion if I'd let any other man than myself kill that swine. But now, when I meet him, I can look him in the face, and we can laugh together. He was always a great fellow for laughin', was Jerry, Mostly laughing at me, or somebody else. But he was always laughing. I'll bet that he's cracking his sides, as he looks down here and sees Loomis lying stretched out!"

He slumped over a little to one side. Carr with his great hands straightened Ferrald gently again.

Ferrald looked up and said suddenly: "Chief, what you think of the old boy, eh? Still shoots 'em straight, eh?"

"Jim, you saved me. You and Carr saved us all! A pair of you against all of them!"

"I don't mind about the saving. I'd as soon that everybody was going along with me," said Ferrald. "What I mean is the shooting. Firelight ain't so pretty for shooting, either. There's too much wabble to it. But I want you to look over yonder for a sawed-off chunk of a brute that looked like Lefty Payson to me. See if he ain't got a bullet between the eyes, because that's where I aimed to plant him. Firelight shooting, Chief. Remember that it was done by firelight."

"You're the best rifle shot that I ever saw," said the Chief, getting down on one knee before Ferrald.

Ferrald laughed like an embarrassed girl.

"Aw, quit kidding me," said he.

"The best rifle shot I ever saw—for rapid fire, I mean," said the Chief.

"You mean that?" whispered Ferrald.

"I mean it," said the Chief.

Ferrald went all to pieces. The cigarette twisted in his fingers. The burning butt of it scorched his flesh, but he couldn't feel the pain. I knocked the cigarette away. His hand lay on the ground all doubled up, as though the wrist were broken.

"Don't lay me down, yet, Carr," said Ferrald, whispering. "Listen to me, Chief."

"I'm listening," said the Chief.

"You'll tell 'em about the rifle work, will you?" asked Ferrald.

"I'll tell everybody. I'm going to have it printed. I'm going to have it printed in a magazine—stories about how you could shoot," said the Chief.

Ferrald smiled, and in his weakness, his mouth yawned open a little, which made his smile a bad thing to look at.

"All right, leave me lay down," said Ferrald.

Carr lowered him gently to the ground, and kept one of his big hands tenderly under the head of Jim Ferrald. I can tell you a thing that you won't believe—that this fellow Carr, this giant, this man without fear, had tears rolling down his face. There was something about the way Ferrald had fought and died that weakened him.

Jim Ferrald gasped out: "Ain't Jerry having the laugh of his life now, when he looks down and sees Loomis corked? And I'm goin' to hear the last of his laugh, right now, or else—"

His mouth stayed parted, but the last word did not come out. He was dead.

The reason that this was all written down was mostly because a good many wild yarns were going around, and I wanted to put them right. Some people seemed to think that I had done a regular whirlwind part, but I couldn't let ideas like that get afloat. I've put down just what happened, only filling in, here and there, in conversations, because conversations are pretty hard to remember. But mostly, I've managed to stick to the facts.

Maybe the reputation that I got out of the fracas helped to make life peaceful up there on the Carr ranch in the Blue Waters. The crooks are gone. The end of Loomis was the signal for them to scatter, and you couldn't find a thug anywhere around. If there were one to be found, I suppose that Sting Ray would find him and put an end to him, as he would to any snake. Sting is mostly useful for shooting venison, and keeping Ralph Carr company. Sue is chiefly busy around the children, and Mother and I run the place. She was glad enough to sell out the old ranch and move up here with us, mainly because the Chief has got a job over in the Creston mine, on the near side of Blue Water town. That makes us all close together.

Allardyce is up there with him. They live in a cottage, and she does the cooking and likes it. She's that kind of a girl. The Chief won't let her father even buy her clothes. But they're pretty well-fixed. He's studying at night, and making a regular mining engineer out of himself, and the opinion of Mr. Creston is that he's going to make a humdinger.

But above all, he's useful in handling the men. They

don't have any strikes in the Creston mine. No, sir-ree! Not with the Chief strolling around and keeping an eye on things. Yet I happen to know that he's never put a hand on a gun in years, not even to go hunting. He doesn't need guns to make other people look up to him. His eye is enough, and his smile can stop a brawl.

He came over the other day for the christening of our oldest boy, which was done rather late. We couldn't call the boy "Chief" very well, And nobody hardly knows that the Chief's real name is Herbert. So we called the youngster "Ray," and call him "Sting" for short.

Sting Ray says it's all just a lot of nonsense, but down in the hard heart of him, he's a pleased man. Sting has worked pretty deep with all of us. He's under our skin, and we couldn't do without him. And when I think back to the old days, it makes me smile to look at him, with his double limp, and his smile, and all of that. For though the heart of a man can change, something out of his past seems to stay written in his face.